He brought her ___
you. I'm even glad I lost my memory."

"I'm glad we met, too. But you shouldn't say that about having amnesia."

"It's giving me a chance to start over."

"This isn't starting over, J.D. It's a break from your other life."

"I don't care about my other life."

"You shouldn't say that, either. It's important to care about who you are."

How could he care about something he couldn't remember? They didn't talk anymore, and he was grateful for the silence. He didn't want to disturb the bond. He wanted the luxury of knowing her in this way. He was in the moment. He was part of it. John Doe and Jenna Byrd, he thought.

He danced with her as if his amnesia depended on it, the heat between them surging through his veins.

This was a memory he would never forget.

Dear Reader,

Although I have been writing for Harlequin since 1999, this is my first Special Edition, and I'm thrilled to be part of this wonderful line. *The Texan's Future Bride* is the second book in a three-book miniseries called Byrds of a Feather. The other two authors are Judy Duarte and Crystal Green, who are also my beloved friends and critique partners. We've been reading and critiquing each other's work since the inception of our careers and love each other like family.

Family is the key ingredient in the Byrds of a Feather series. We created a mixed-up brood of Texans who need each other more than they know. During the time Judy, Crystal and I started plotting this series, I was going through a difficult time in my life and just being involved in this project helped me get through it.

In *The Texan's Future Bride,* Jenna Byrd is going through a bit of a rough patch, too, coming to terms with her estranged family and a long-ago feud. And while Jenna is in the midst of this emotional journey, a mysterious cowboy with amnesia appears on the scene, drawing her into his troubled heart.

Enter J.D. (John Doe) and let the happily-ever-after begin....

Hugs and love,

Sheri

THE TEXAN'S FUTURE BRIDE

SHERI WHITEFEATHER

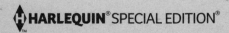 HARLEQUIN® SPECIAL EDITION®

Recycling programs
for this product may
not exist in your area.

ISBN-13: 978-0-373-65738-4

THE TEXAN'S FUTURE BRIDE

Copyright © 2013 by Sheree Henry-Whitefeather

This edition published by arrangement with Harlequin Books S.A.

For questions and comments about the quality of this book, please contact us at CustomerService@Harlequin.com.

® and TM are trademarks of Harlequin Enterprises Limited or its corporate affiliates. Trademarks indicated with ® are registered in the United States Patent and Trademark Office, the Canadian Trade Marks Office and in other countries.

HARLEQUIN®
™ www.Harlequin.com

SHERI WHITEFEATHER

is a bestselling author who has won numerous awards, including readers' and reviewers' choice honors. She writes a variety of romance novels for Harlequin Books. She has become known for incorporating Native American elements into her stories. She has two grown children who are tribally enrolled members of the Muscogee Creek Nation.

Sheri is of Italian-American descent. Her great-grandparents immigrated to the United States from Italy through Ellis Island, originating from Castel di Sangro and Sicily. She lives in California and enjoys ethnic dining, shopping in vintage stores and going to art galleries and museums. Sheri loves to hear from her readers. Visit her website at www.SheriWhiteFeather.com.

To Judy Duarte and Crystal Green for supporting
my dreams and always believing that they will come true.

Chapter One

What the—?

As Jenna Byrd steered her truck toward the Flying B, she noticed a man walking along the private road that led to the ranch. Or stumbling was more like it. He didn't look familiar, but he didn't seem out of place, either. His dusty jeans, plain T-shirt and battered boots were typical small-town Texas attire. He was missing a hat, though. Had he lost it somewhere? His short dark hair was decidedly messy.

Jenna frowned. Clearly, he was snockered in the middle of the day. Cowboys could be a hell-raisin' breed. Of course she didn't dally with that kind. Although she was hoping to find a cowboy to call her own, she was attracted to well-behaved men, not rabble-rousers who could barely put one foot in front of the other. He was ambling toward her pickup instead of away from it.

Good grief. She couldn't just leave him out here. The Flying B was about five miles down the road, and in his condition, he would never make it. And why he was heading toward the ranch was beyond her.

She stopped her truck and sighed. She knew he wasn't a Flying B employee. She'd made a point of meeting everyone on the payroll. Jenna owned a portion of the ranch. She and her sister and their cousin had inherited equal shares of the Flying B, and they were going to turn it into a B and B.

She rolled down her window and said, "What are you doing out here?"

He looked at her as if he wasn't really seeing her. His deep brown eyes were glazed. He didn't respond.

She repeated the question.

He blinked at her. He was probably around her age, thirty or so, with tanned skin and striking features— handsome, even in his wasted state.

Curious, she tried to figure him out. Maybe he was a whiskey-toting hitchhiker. Or maybe he was affiliated with another ranch in the area and after he'd tied one on, he'd mistakenly taken the wrong road. There had to an explanation for his disorderly presence.

Hoping to solve the dilemma, she asked, "Who are you?"

"Who are you?" he parroted.

This was going nowhere. "You've had too much to drink."

He squinted. "I have?"

"Yes."

"I don't think so."

Easy for him to say. He was too drunk to know the

difference. While she debated how to handle the situation, he staggered a little more.

"I feel funny," he said.

No kidding, she thought.

"I've got a headache." He rubbed the back of his head. When he brought his fingers forward, the tips were red.

Her pulse jumped. He was bleeding.

She parked and leaped out of her truck. Had he gotten into a brawl? Overly intoxicated men were prone to that sort of behavior. But whatever he'd done, it didn't matter. All that mattered was getting his wound treated.

"My cousin's fiancé is a doctor. He lives at the ranch where I live, and I think he's home today. If he isn't, I'll take you to his office."

"No. That's okay." He wiped his hands on his pants. "I'm better now."

Obviously, he wasn't. She slipped her arm around him and realized that he didn't smell of alcohol. Most likely, he hadn't been drinking, which made his condition a bigger cause for concern. He was probably dazed because of the injury.

"Come on. Let's get you into the truck."

Shouldering his weight wasn't easy. He was about six feet, packed with lean muscle mass. At five-five, with a slight build, she was no match for him.

He lagged against her, and she held him tighter. Nonetheless, he kept insisting that he was fine, which clearly wasn't the case. He was definitely confused.

Once he was seated, she eased away from him and closed the door. She got behind the wheel and reached for her cell phone. She called Mike Sanchez or "Doc" as he'd become known in these parts. He was at the ranch. She asked him to meet her at the main house and told him that she was bringing an injured man with her.

"The back of his head is bleeding." She glanced at her passenger. He was staring out the window with those glazed eyes. She lowered her voice. "I don't know much about these things, but I think he has some sort of concussion. I found him wandering along Flying B Road."

"Don't worry, Jenna," Doc replied. "Just stay calm and get him here."

"I'm on my way." She ended the call, then started the engine and headed for her destination.

The cowboy turned to look at her. "Are we on a date?"

Yikes. Talk about befuddled. His condition was worse than she thought. "I'm taking you to see a doctor, remember?"

"Your hair is pretty." He reached out as if he meant to grasp a loose tendril of her wavy gold locks.

Jenna's heartbeat skittered. He didn't make contact, but she could almost imagine how his tortured touch would feel.

Almost. She focused on the road.

"Very pretty," he said.

She gripped the wheel, and to keep him from reaching for her hair again, she redirected his thoughts.

"What's your name?" she asked, rephrasing her original "Who are you?" question.

He furrowed his brows. It wasn't a trick question, but he didn't appear capable of a response. He didn't know his own name.

"It's okay," she said. "That's why I'm taking you to see a doctor." Besides, all they had to do was look at his ID to see who he was. Everyone carried identification with them. Still, not knowing something as simple as his name wasn't a good sign.

He leaned against the window, then closed his eyes. She hoped that he wasn't going to pass out. That wouldn't be a good sign, either.

She increased her speed, bumping along the road, her truck flanked by green pastures and grazing cattle.

Finally, as the main house came into view, she breathed a sigh of "thank You, God" relief.

The dashing young doctor was waiting for her on the wraparound porch. Tammy, her equally fetching cousin, was there, too. Jenna had only met Tammy recently, when all of the inheritance whoopla had begun. None of the heirs had grown up on the Flying B or visited when they were kids because their families had been estranged from each other. So, when they'd gotten called to their ailing grandpa's bedside, and when he'd died, they'd wept for a man they'd just begun to know.

She glanced at the cowboy beside her. Now wasn't the time to think about men she barely knew. Or death. Or anything bad.

Jenna stopped the truck, and Doc opened the passenger side and escorted the patient into the house.

Once Jenna exited the vehicle, Tammy approached her, and they went inside, too.

Doc didn't waste time. He was already examining the stranger, who sat on the edge of a sturdy leather sofa, looking as confused as ever.

Jenna stood back and frowned. "Do you recognize him?" she asked Tammy. "Do you know if he's from around here?"

"No."

"Me, either." But dang if he didn't make her tongue stick to the roof of her mouth. She couldn't get his tortured attempt to touch her out of her mind.

Just a few feet away, Doc was telling the patient that he was going to need a couple of stitches. In fact, Doc was preparing to patch him up. But the cut itself was incidental. What obviously concerned Doc were his other symptoms.

Apparently Jenna was right. Indeed, he had a concussion.

Thing was, his identity was still unknown. He wasn't carrying any form of identification; Doc checked his person.

"What do you think is going to happen?" Jenna whispered to Tammy.

"I don't know."

Neither did Jenna. But it was clear from the examination that he had no recollection about himself or how he'd gotten hurt.

After his cut was sanitized and stitched, Doc made arrangements for him to be treated at the local hospital. He spoke gently to the patient, then explained the situation to Jenna.

"I'm going to order a CT scan," he said. "At this point, it's impossible to know the severity of his trauma."

"What's the worst-case scenario?" she asked, making sure the stranger was out of earshot.

"Bleeding in the brain."

She shivered.

Doc concluded, "But let's not get ahead of ourselves. Let's get a thorough diagnosis first."

"I want to go to the hospital with him." She was unable to bear the thought of abandoning him.

"That's fine. A police report will have to be filed, too, since we don't know who he is or what triggered the injury. He'll be admitted as a John Doe."

Jenna didn't like the impersonal sound of that. But she didn't like any of this. She preferred to have her ducks in a tidy yellow row, with carefully laid plans, no matter what aspect of her life it concerned. She'd even created a list of the type of qualities she wanted her future husband to have, a man who would be nothing like her father. She used to be disappointed in her dad, but these days she was downright ashamed of him. A humiliating skeleton in his closet had surfaced.

She glanced at the stranger. Did he have skeletons in his closet, too? Even if he did, it was none of her concern. She was going to see him through this injury and forget about him.

Doc and Tammy took him to the hospital, and Jenna followed them in her truck.

She sat in the waiting room while he underwent the CT scan. Was she going to be able to forget about him? Already she was feeling oddly attached, as if she was responsible for him somehow.

She glanced over at Tammy, who occupied the seat next to her. "Thanks for keeping me company."

"It shouldn't take long. Rather than wait for a written report, Mike is going to look at the scans himself, along with the radiologist, of course."

"It's nice having a doctor in the family."

Tammy quirked a smile. "Very nice." She stood up. "Do you want some coffee?"

"Sure."

"How do you take it?"

"Cream and sugar."

"Coming right up."

Jenna watched her cousin head for the vending machine. She was a petite brunette, thriving on newfound love. She and Jenna formed a bond when Jenna had helped her with a makeover that had caught the doctor's eye. Tammy was a tomboy turned hot tamale. She could still ride and rope with the best of 'em, but she also looked darn fine in feminine attire. The girl could cook up a storm, too. Soon the Flying B cook would be retiring and Tammy would be taking over as the down-home B and B chef.

Tammy returned with two cups and handed Jenna one. She took a sip. It tasted better than expected.

Jenna said about the stranger, "I can't help but wonder who he is. What his name is, what his family is like."

"Hopefully he'll remember soon."

"I just hope the scan comes out all right." She drank a bit more of her coffee. "He said some weird things when we were in the truck. He told me that he liked my hair, then he asked me if we were on a date."

"That must have been awkward."

"It was." She frowned. "What sort of treatment do they do if someone is bleeding in the brain?"

"I have no idea, but you shouldn't be dwelling on that."

"I know. But I'm the one who found him."

"Finders keepers, losers weepers?" Tammy put her cup beside a dog-eared magazine. "Did you ever say that when you were a kid?"

"All the time. But I hope that doesn't apply to this situation."

"Like someone is left behind weeping for him?"

Jenna nodded, and they both fell silent. But it seemed better not to talk. Other people had just entered the waiting room with somber looks on their faces, as if they were afraid that they might be left weeping for whoever they were there to see.

Time ticked by.

Then Tammy looked up and said, "There's Mike," as her fiancé strode toward them.

Jenna got to her feet, with Tammy on her heels.

Doc said to them, "The results were normal, but we're going to keep him overnight for observation."

"Then what?" Jenna asked.

"Then we'll reevaluate his condition in the morning."

"Do you think his memory will return by then?"

"It's possible. Oftentimes these sorts of lapses only last a day or two. But it could continue for a while. It's hard to say."

"Can I see him?"

"Once we check him into a room, you can visit him."

By the time that happened, the stranger was asleep. Doc and Tammy went home, and Jenna sat in a stiff plastic chair beside his bed and watched him. She used the opportunity to study his features: dark eyebrows, a strong, sharp nose, cheekbones a male model would envy, medium-size lips with a bit of a downward slant. That made her curious about his smile. Was it bright? Crooked? Brooding? She noticed that he was harboring a five-o'clock shadow. The sexy scruff made him look even more like the cowboy she assumed he was.

The hospital gown, however, didn't; it robbed him of his edge.

He stirred in his sleep, and she frowned. Although he had a semiprivate room and the curtain was drawn, the TV of the older man next to him sounded in her ears. A game show was playing, a program that had been on the air since she was a kid. She'd never actually seen it, not all the way through. But she'd gotten used to hearing the noisy show in the background when her dad used to watch it, much like she was hearing it now.

Tuning out the sound, she studied the stranger again. Because she was tempted to skim his cheek and feel the warmth of his skin, she kept her hands on her lap. She even curled her fingers to keep them still. Being this close to him while he slept wasn't a good idea. She should go home, but she stayed for as long as the hospital would allow, already anxious to return the following day.

In the morning, Jenna had breakfast with her sister in the main house, surrounded by retro-style gingham accents in the kitchen. Unfortunately it was too early to head over to the hospital. With the exception of spouses and significant others, visiting hours were limited.

She'd barely slept last night, wondering if the stranger would recoup his memory today.

She glanced across the table at Donna, but her sister didn't look up. She was busy texting, in between sips of fresh-brewed coffee and bites of a Spanish omelet, courtesy of the soon-to-retire cook.

Jenna continued to study Donna. They'd always been different from each other. Jenna, a certified horseback riding instructor, loved everything country, and Donna, a magazine writer turned marketer, loved everything city. As soon as the B and B was off the ground, Donna would be returning to New York, where she lived and worked. Jenna, on the other hand, planned to stay at the ranch and help run the B and B with Tammy.

Donna finally glanced up. "What?" she said.

"Nothing."

"Then why were you staring at me?"

"I was just thinking about how opposite we are."

"We're siblings, not clones."

"Yes, but you'd think that we would have more in common. Or look more alike or whatever." Although both were blonde, Donna was a year older, three inches taller and wildly curvy. She had the figure of a 1940s pinup, while Jenna was small and lean.

Donna shrugged and went back to texting, and Jenna considered how distant their relationship was. Her sister had trouble connecting with people on an emotional level, but Jenna could hardly blame her. They'd been raised in a go-your-own-way environment.

Tammy entered the room, and Jenna immediately said, "Hi."

"Hello, yourself." Their cousin sat down and greeted Donna, as well. Then she turned back to Jenna and said, "Mike left a couple of hours ago to check on our patient."

Her stomach fluttered. "He did? Any word?"

"From Mike? No. But I'm sure he'll call when he can."

Donna quit texting. "What patient? Who's sick?"

Jenna answered, "I found a man yesterday. He was wandering around on the road with a concussion." She went on to explain the details. "Hopefully he'll be better today."

"Wow," Donna said. "Can you imagine losing your memory?"

No, but Jenna wouldn't mind forgetting about the mess their dad had made of things. But he'd been notorious for disappointing her, even when she was a child. He'd never been there when she needed him. He'd been too busy with his corporate job. He rarely attended parent-teacher conferences or planned birthday parties or took his daughters to the movies or engaged in the types of activities that would have made them seem more like a family.

She glanced at Donna. Funny thing about her sister. Before the skeleton in Dad's closet had surfaced, Donna used to idolize him. He'd been her hero, the person she often emulated, particularly with her workaholic, career-is-king habits. Not that Donna would ever admit how deeply he influenced her. But Jenna was keenly aware of it.

Clearing the Dad-clutter from her mind, Jenna said to Tammy, "I was planning on going to the hospital later, but maybe I should wait for Mike to call."

"It might take him a while to check in," her cousin replied. "He has a lot of rounds to make. Why don't you head over to the hospital now and look in on the man? I can tell you're still worried about him."

"I can't see him until noon."

"Says who?"

"The hospital visiting hours."

Tammy waved away the rules. "They probably won't notice if you slip in a little early."

"I think it would be better if I went at noon." She

wasn't comfortable taking liberties. She preferred to play by the book.

Tammy didn't push her out of her comfort zone and neither did Donna. They allowed her to be her regimented self.

When the time rolled around for her to get ready, she donned classic Western wear: a broomstick skirt, a feminine blouse and a nice pair of boots. She freshened up her face and fluffed her hair, too. Not that it should matter what the stranger thought of her appearance. If he was better today, this would probably be the last time she saw him.

She arrived at the hospital at twelve o'clock sharp and went to the nurses' station, where she inquired about the patient's condition. They informed her that he was awake and coherent, and once everything was in order, Dr. Sanchez would be releasing him.

So, he *was* better.

She thanked them for the information and continued down the hall. A moment later, she stalled. She was nervous about conversing with him.

Pushing past the trepidation, she proceeded. She entered his room and passed the TV-watching patient. Today he was engaged in a sitcom from the seventies. He didn't glance her way, and she left him alone, too.

She moved forward and came face-to-face with the stranger. He was sitting up in bed. His gaze zeroed in on hers, and her heart went bumpy.

"Good morning," she said, keeping a calm voice.

"You're the girl from yesterday."

"Yes."

"The blonde I thought I was dating. I'm sorry about that."

Dang. Did he have to go and mention it? "It's okay. You were out of it."

He nodded, and she took the seat next to his bed, the same spot where she'd watched him sleep. "You look healthier." Still a bit worn-out, she thought, but an improvement nonetheless. "I heard that Doc will be releasing you."

"Yes, but I'm supposed to take it easy."

"You can't go kicking up your heels just yet?"

"No. Not yet." He smiled a little.

It was sinfully crooked. The *bump-bump* in her chest returned. "I'm Jenna, by the way. Jenna Byrd."

"Thank you for what you did. Jenna," he added softly.

The bumping intensified. "I'm glad I was there to help." She scooted to the edge of her chair. "So, what's your name?"

He furrowed his dark brows. "I don't know. I still can't remember anything, aside from you bringing me to your ranch and coming here."

She gaped at him. "Your memory hasn't recovered? Then why is Doc releasing you?"

"Because I'm not dizzy or confused, and my vital signs are good. I have what's called retrograde amnesia, but they can't keep me in the hospital for that. Besides, my memories are supposed to return. It's just a matter of when."

She didn't know what to say. He was still as much of a stranger as he was before.

He said, "The sheriff was here earlier. He took a report. He took my fingerprints, too." He held up his hands and gazed at them. "If I'm in the system, they'll be able to identify me that way."

He might have a criminal record? That wasn't a comforting thought. "Do you think you're in the system?"

"I don't know." He lowered his hands. "But the sheriff doesn't want Dr. Sanchez to release me until the results are in. So we're waiting to hear. I guess the police want to be sure that there isn't a warrant out for my arrest before they put me back on the streets."

"Do you mind if I wait until you hear something?"

"Why would you want to do that?"

Because she still felt responsible for him. Or was it because she was so doggone attracted to him? That wasn't a comforting thought, either. Confused and covering her tracks she said, "I'm interested in knowing who you are." And hoping that he was an upstanding guy.

"At the moment, I'm no one."

"That's not true. Everyone is someone."

He glanced away. Obviously her comment hadn't made a dent in his amnesiac armor. She wanted to reassure him, but how could she, especially since he might be wanted by the police?

Just then, double sets of footsteps sounded, and Jenna turned around in her chair. The stranger shifted in the direction of the approaching people, too.

It was Doc, making a crisp-white presentation in his lab coat, and next to him was a tall, stocky lawman.

As the air grew thick with anticipation, the stranger shot Jenna a quick glance.

Trapping her in the moment they'd been waiting for.

Chapter Two

Amid the silence, Doc caught Jenna's attention. She expected him to ask her to leave, but he merely nodded an acknowledgment. Maybe it was going to be okay. Maybe there was nothing to be concerned about.

The lawman said to the patient, "I'm Deputy Tobbs. The sheriff assigned your case to me."

"Do I have a record?" the stranger asked bluntly.

The deputy shifted his weight. "No, you don't. Your fingerprints aren't on file, but I'm going to investigate further. I'll do my best to uncover your identity and discover what happened to you. I'll be questioning everyone in the area, in case you work around here or were visiting someone."

"Someone who hasn't noticed that I'm gone?"

"It could have been a surprise visit and you never made it to your destination. It could have been a number of things. I'm inclined to think that you were assaulted and robbed, possibly carjacked, which would account for you wandering around on foot. But we'll have to wait and see what turns up."

The stranger tugged a hand through his hair, stopping short of his injury. "It could be worse, I guess." He addressed Doc. "Are you going to sign my release papers now?"

"Yes, but first we need to figure out where you're going to go."

The stranger replied, "Is there a homeless shelter in the area?"

The deputy answered the question. "There's one in the next county, about thirty miles from here."

"Then that will have to do, if they'll take me."

"I can give them a call," the deputy said.

No way, Jenna thought. She wasn't going to let him go off like that. She would worry about him. Still, did she have a right to intervene? Regardless, she couldn't seem to hold back.

She said to the stranger, "You can stay at the Flying B until you regain your memory or until Deputy Tobbs finds out who you are. We're turning the ranch into a B and B, and we have guest rooms and cabins on the property."

"I can't stay there."

Jenna persisted, especially now that she'd made up her mind about saving him, or whatever it was she was trying to do. "Why not?"

"I just can't. I shouldn't."

"Sure you can," Doc said, supporting her idea. "It would be a good place for you to recover."

"I don't know."

Jenna frowned. "What's not to know? Just say yes."

He frowned, too. "Are you always this insistent?"

Was she? "Sometimes." Considering from the time that she and Donna were kids, the one lesson their father had always taught was to go after what they wanted. "But Doc agrees with me, so you're outnumbered."

"Consider it part of your treatment," Doc said. "I could keep a better eye on you, and being surrounded by fresh air would be a heck of a lot nicer than being holed in a homeless shelter."

The deputy interjected. "Sounds like you've got it worked out."

"We do," Jenna assured him.

"Then I'm going to take my leave." He placed his card on the rolling stand beside the bed. "Call me if you have any questions," he told the man with amnesia. "And if I need to reach you, I'll stop by the Flying B." The deputy turned to Jenna. "You should introduce him to everyone at the ranch. It's possible that someone there will recognize him."

"I will, just as soon as he's feeling up to it."

He turned back to the patient. "You take care."

"Thank you," came the polite reply.

Deputy Tobbs said goodbye to everyone and left the room, a hush forming in his absence. Jenna wondered if Doc was going to depart, too. But he stayed quietly put.

She said to the stranger, "You're going to need another name, other than John Doe."

His dark gaze caught hers. "Some people have that name for real."

"I know. But it's doubtful that you do."

"Then you can pick one."

"You want me to name you?"

"Somebody has to."

Jenna glanced at Doc. He stood off to the side, clutching a clipboard that probably contained "John Doe's" charts. Anxious, she crossed her arms over her chest. Doc's silent observation created a fishbowl-type effect. But he had a right to analyze his patient's reactions.

Was he analyzing her, too?

She'd been bothered by the John Doe reference from the beginning, but now that she'd been given the responsibility of changing it, she felt an enormous amount of pressure.

Could Doc tell how nervous she was?

She asked the stranger, "Are you sure you don't want to come up with something yourself?"

"I'm positive."

He sounded as if it didn't matter, that with or without a makeshift name, he still considered himself no one.

Reminding her of how lost he truly was.

As he waited for the outcome, he thought about how surreal all of this was. He felt like a ketchup jar someone had banged upside the counter, with memories locked inside that wouldn't come out.

Emptiness. Nothingness.

His only lifeline was the pretty blonde beside his bed and the doctor watching the scene unfold.

"What do you think of J.D.?" she asked.

"The initials for John Doe?"

She nodded. "I always thought that using initials in place of a name was sexy."

He started. Was she serious? "Sexy?"

She blushed, her cheeks turning a soft shade of pink. "I didn't mean it like that."

Intrigued, he tilted his head. She'd gone from being aggressive to downright shy. "How did you mean it?"

"That it's mysterious."

"Then I guess it fits." Everything was a mystery, right down to his confusion about dating her. Was she the type he would've dated in the past? Or did he even have a type?

"So we can start calling you J.D. now?" she asked, obviously double-checking.

He nodded.

"And you're going to stay at the Flying B?"

He nodded again, still feeling reluctant about being her houseguest or cabin guest or whatever. As far as he was concerned, a homeless shelter would have sufficed.

She said, "When I first saw you, I assumed that you were a cowboy, maybe an employee of a neighboring ranch. I hadn't considered a carjacking, but I wondered if you might be a hitchhiker. I'm glad the deputy is going to talk to everyone in the area about you. Then we'll know for sure." She glanced at his clothes, which were hanging nearby. "You were certainly dressed like a local cowboy, except that you didn't have a hat. But I figured that you'd lost it somewhere."

He followed her line of sight. The T-shirt, jeans and worn-out boots he'd been wearing were as unfamiliar as the day he'd been born. "I don't have a recollection of doing ranch work."

"You don't have a recollection of anything," she reminded him.

"I know, but wouldn't I have a feeling of being connected to ranching? Wouldn't it be ingrained in me if that's what I did for a living?" He turned to the expert. "What do you think, Dr. Sanchez?"

"I think it's too soon to be concerned about that. You just need to rest and let your feelings fall into place when they're meant to." He smiled. "I also think you should start calling me Doc."

"Okay, Doc." He preferred less formality, too, and already he'd gotten used to hearing Jenna say it. A moment later, he shifted his gaze back to his unfamiliar clothes.

Jenna said, "You put some miles on those boots."

"I must have thought they were comfortable." He noticed that the toes were starting to turn up. "I guess I'm going to find out if I still like wearing them."

"Yes, J.D., you are," Doc said, using his new name. "In fact, you can get dressed now, if you want. I can send a nurse in if you need help."

"No, I can handle it."

"All right. Then I'll go get your papers ready, and Jenna can step out of the room and come back when you're done."

J.D. got a highly inappropriate urge, wishing that he could ask her to stay and help him get dressed. He even imagined her hand on his zipper.

Hell and damnation.

He should have insisted on going to a shelter. Clearly, being around Jenna wasn't a good idea.

She and the doctor left, closing the curtain behind them. J.D. got out of bed and walked over to the closet, still thinking about Jenna.

He cursed quietly under his breath, stripped off the hospital gown and put on his Western wear. He grappled with his belt. He fought the boots, too. They felt odd at first, but he got used to them soon enough.

Curious to look at himself in the mirror, he went into

the bathroom. He didn't recognize his reflection, with him wearing the clothes. He was still a nowhere man.

Luckily, the hospital had provided a few necessities, like a comb, toothpaste and a toothbrush. Still standing in front of the mirror, he combed his hair straight back, but it fell forward naturally, so he let it be. They hadn't provided a razor, so he had no choice but to leave the beard stubble. It was starting to itch and he wanted it gone. Or maybe it was the image it created that he didn't like. It made him look as haunted as he felt, like an Old West outlaw.

J.D. the Kid? No. He wasn't a kid. He figured himself for early thirties. Or that was how he appeared. But he could be mistaken.

Blowing out a breath, he returned to his room and opened the curtain, letting Jenna know that she could come back.

She did, about five minutes later, bringing two cups of coffee with her.

"It's from the vending machine," she said. "But it's pretty good. I had some last night when I was waiting for your test results." She handed him a cup. "It has cream and sugar. I hope that's okay."

"It's fine. Thanks. I don't have a preference, not that I'm aware of, anyway." He sat on the edge of the bed, offering her the chair. "You've been putting in a lot of time at this place, hanging out for a man you barely know."

"I'm starting to get to know you." She smiled. "You obviously like coffee."

"So it seems." He drank it right down. "I had orange juice with breakfast, but this hits the spot."

"We have gourmet coffeemakers in the guest cabins. You can brew yourself a fancy cup of Joe tomorrow morning."

"That sounds good, but maybe I shouldn't stay there. You don't need the burden of having a guy like me around."

"You can't back out. You already agreed. Doctor's orders, remember?"

Yes, but his recovery didn't include the stirrings she incited. Even now, he wanted to see her blush again. He liked the shy side of her.

"When this is over, I'll repay you for your hospitality," he said.

"Just get better, okay? That will be payment enough."

"You're a nice girl, Jenna."

"And you seem like a nice man."

"You thought I was drunk off my butt when you saw me stumbling around. I remember you telling me that I had too much to drink."

"I retracted that when I saw that your head was bleeding. How is your head, by the way?"

"Still hurts a little."

"How about your feet?"

He squinted. "My feet aren't injured."

"I was talking about your boots. How do they feel?"

Oh, yeah. The boots. He glanced down at the scuffed leather. "Fine." He motioned to hers. "You've got yourself a fancy pair."

"These are my dressy ones. Sometimes I go dancing in them, too."

"I have no idea if I know how to dance."

"You can try the two-step and see."

"Right now?" He teased her. "Up and down the hospital corridor?"

She laughed. "Later, smarty, when you're up to par."

Were they flirting? It sure as heck seemed as if they were. But it didn't last long because he didn't let it.

He knew better than to start something that he was in no position to finish. She seemed to know it, too. She turned off the charm at the same instant he did.

Tempering what was happening between them.

As a bright and bouncy nurse wheeled J.D. out to Jenna's truck, he said, "I'd rather walk."

"It's hospital policy," the chipper lady said. "Everyone leaves in a wheelchair."

He made a face, and Jenna smiled to herself. Machismo. He certainly behaved like a cowboy.

She stopped smiling. She was actually taking this man home with her, and she knew darn well that he was as attracted to her as she was to him.

But they weren't going to act on it. They were both cautious enough not to let it take over. So it would be fine, she assured herself. He would be a recuperating guest, a patient of Doc's, and nothing more.

She turned on the radio, and they listened to music instead of talking.

Finally, when they were on the private road leading to the ranch, he glanced over at her and said, "Déjà vu," making a joke about repeating his car-ride experience from yesterday.

She tried to make light of it, too. "Your first encounter with it."

"That I'm able to remember. I probably had déjà vu in my old life."

His old life. That made it sound as if he'd become someone new. She supposed that, at least for now, he was a different person. But since she didn't know who he was before, she couldn't compare the old with the new.

"I wonder if I should put you in the dream cabin."

"The cabins have names? Is that part of the B and B thing?"

"No. The dream cabin is what everyone on the ranch has been calling it, for years, amongst themselves. So we call it that, too. It has an old feather bed that used to belong to our great-grandmother. She had the gift of second sight, and her visions came in the form of dreams while she was sleeping in it."

"Interesting family history."

"The bed is magical."

He openly disagreed. "Your great-granny having visions in the bed doesn't make it magical."

"Other people have had vision-type dreams while sleeping in it, too. Tammy had dreams about Doc. Then later, he had a life-altering dream about her, and he wasn't even at the cabin when it happened to him. But we figured that her dreams triggered his, so the feather bed was still part of it."

"Maybe you shouldn't put me in that cabin."

"Why? Don't you want to have a dream that might come true?"

"It just seems like something that should stay within your family."

"Doc wasn't in our family until he and Tammy got engaged."

"I'm not going to get engaged to anyone."

Their discussion was barreling down an uncomfortable path. She struggled to rein it back in. "I wasn't insinuating that you were."

"I don't understand the point of me sleeping in the bed."

"You might have a dream that will help you regain your memory."

"I can't imagine that."

She parked in front of the main house. "Anything is possible. Wait here and I'll get the key to the cabin." She went inside, wondering why he wasn't more interested in the bed. Didn't he want to regain his memory?

She returned with the key, and he sat in the passenger seat, looking tired and confused.

He said, "I don't mean to offend you, Jenna, but I don't know if I believe in magic."

Ah, so that was it. He was a skeptic. "You just need to recover, J.D. and let the rest of it happen naturally."

"Magic isn't natural."

"I didn't used to think so, either. But I've become open-minded about it since Tammy and Doc had their dreams."

He didn't respond, but it was just as well. She didn't want to discuss the details of Doc and Tammy's romance with him.

She took him to the cabin. They went inside, and she showed him around.

"This place was locked up for a long time," she said. "But we aired it out and put some modern appliances in it."

"Like the gourmet coffeemaker?"

She nodded. "Eventually we're going to use it as one of the rental cabins. We think people will be fascinated by the magic associated with the bed. Of course we can't guarantee that they'll dream while they're here."

"You can't make that guarantee for me, either."

"No, but I think it's worth a shot."

They entered the bedroom, and since the bed had already been presented as a focal point, it stood out like a sore thumb, even though it had been designed to look soft and inviting. The quilt was a soft chocolate-brown, with a sheepskin throw draped across it.

He ran his hand across the sheepskin. "Have you ever slept here?"

A sinful chill raced up her spine. Suddenly she was imagining sleeping there with him. "No."

"If you believe in the bed's magic, why haven't you tried it yourself?"

"There's nothing I need to dream about. Besides, there's another story about someone who stayed here that's been bothering me."

He frowned. "Who?

Jenna winced. She should have kept her mouth shut. "Someone named Savannah Jeffries. She was my uncle's girlfriend when they were younger." She was also the woman who'd had a scandalous tryst with Jenna's father, but she wasn't about to mention that part.

"Did she dream while she was here?"

"I don't know. Tammy accidentally discovered a secret Savannah was keeping, though, and now my family has been talking about hiring a P.I. to search for her."

"Why? Did she go missing?" He wrinkled his forehead. "Was there foul play involved?"

"No. She left town on her own. When Tammy first discovered her secret, all of us girls—Tammy, my sister Donna and I—tried to find out things about her on the internet, but nothing turned up."

"Sounds like you want to find her."

"I'm curious about her, but I'd just as soon let sleeping dogs lie." She purposely changed the subject. She wasn't prepared to discuss Savannah's secret or the possible ramifications of it. "Doc will have my hide if I don't let you rest, so I'm going to get going. But I'll come back and bring you something to eat. I'll bring some extra groceries and stock the fridge for future meals, too. Oh, and I'll see if I can drum up some clothes that will fit you." She motioned to his rugged ensemble. "You're going to need more than one shirt and one pair of jeans."

"You don't have to fuss over me."

"I don't mind."

"You're going above and beyond."

"I want you to get well." She left her cell-phone number on the desk. "Call if you need anything."

"How long are you going to be gone?"

"Probably a couple of hours. You should try to nap while I'm gone." She walked to the door and glanced over her shoulder at him.

He stood beside the feather bed, looking like a man in need of magic.

Chapter Three

After Jenna left, J.D. didn't know what to do with himself. He didn't want to take a nap, even if he was supposed to be resting. He glanced around the room, then
eyed the landline phone.

Already he felt like calling Jenna and telling her that
he needed something. But what?

Companionship, he thought. He was lonely as hell.

He sat on the bed, then went ahead and reclined on
it. Damn. The feather mattress was heavenly.

J.D. considered his whereabouts. He was hellishly
lonely on a heavenly bed? Talk about an odd combi-
nation.

The amnesia was odd, too. He couldn't remember
anything about himself, but he knew what year it was,
who was president, what the world at large was like.

He closed his eyes, and unable to resist the bed, he dozed off.

He awakened hours later, the red-digit clock glaring at him. He hadn't dreamed. His subconscious hadn't created any thoughts or images.

He got up and waited for Jenna to return.

She arrived with a light knock at the door. He answered her summons eagerly.

Her hands were filled with grocery bags.

"I'll take those." He lifted the bags and carried them to the kitchen.

She went out to her truck and came back with containers of fried chicken and mashed potatoes.

"I'm not much of a cook," she said. "This came from the diner in town. I picked it up when I got the groceries."

"I hope you're going to join me. It looks like there's plenty for both of us."

"Sure. I'll eat with you." She walked into the dining room to set the table.

After the plates and silverware were in place, she returned to her truck for the rest of the stuff she'd promised. He could see her from his vantage point in the kitchen.

Upon reentering the house, she called out to him. "The clothes belong to a ranch hand who, I think, is about your size. I'll put them on the sofa for you. There's a nice little satchel with toiletries, too. Donna had them made up for the guest rooms and cabins. She's handling the marketing end of the B and B. She's been redecorating, too."

Interested in talking to her, he crammed the grocery bags in the fridge and met her in the dining room.

"What do you do, Jenna?"

"I'm a horseback riding instructor. It was my profession before I came to the Flying B. I've always been a country girl, even when I lived in the city. I grew up in Houston."

"I assumed you grew up here."

"No. Tammy, Donna and I inherited the ranch from our grandfather, and Tammy's brothers inherited some undeveloped land on the west side of the property. All of us were rewarded money, too, with stipulations of how it's to be used. The girls are supposed to keep the ranch going, which we decided includes the inception of the B and B. And the boys are supposed to take advantage of the mineral rights that go with the land, so they'll be commissioning a survey. Our grandfather left us a portion of his legacy, but we barely got to know him before he passed away. Our families were estranged from him and each other."

They sat down to eat. Curious, he asked, "Who was estranged, exactly?"

"Our dads. They're twin brothers. They hadn't spoken to each other or to Grandpa since..."

She didn't finish her statement, and he wondered if the rift had something to do with Savannah Jeffries and why she'd left town.

He said, "Who knows who my family is or if I even have one."

"Everyone comes from somewhere."

"Yes, but I forgot who they were. I mean, how important can they be?"

"You have a head injury. That's not your fault."

He popped open a soda can. "It still feels personal."

"Your life will be back on track before you know it."

Would it? At this point, he couldn't see past his amnesia. He couldn't imagine who he was. "I fell asleep while you were gone."

Her eyes grew wide. "Did you dream?"

"No."

She seemed disappointed. "Maybe you will tonight."

He didn't reply.

A short time later, they finished their meals and went into the living room. They sat on the sofa, and he checked out the clothes, which consisted of a handful of shirts and a couple of pairs of Wrangler jeans. He noticed a package of unopened boxer shorts, too. "Where did these come from?"

"I bought those at the emporium in town. I took a chance that you wore that type. I took a chance on the size, too." She paused, a sweetly shy expression on her face. "I hope it wasn't too forward of me." She quickly added, "I got you socks, too. Did you see those?"

"Yes, thank you." But buying him socks wasn't nearly as intimate as buying him boxers. "I appreciate everything you've been doing for me."

"I borrowed the clothes before I went into town, and then, while I was shopping for groceries, it hit me that you might need those other things, so I made a quick trip to the emporium."

"I feel badly that you've been spending money on me."

"It wasn't that much."

He begged to differ. He knew how expensive it was to live these days. He returned his attention to the clothes, glad they hadn't cost her anything. "These should fit. What's the ranch hand's name who loaned them to me?"

"Caleb Granger. He isn't aware of the loan, though.

He's out of town on a personal matter, but he left some of his things behind."

"You borrowed them without his consent?"

"I didn't. The foreman did. When I mentioned that I needed clothes for someone who was about the same size as Caleb, he went into Caleb's cabin and got them for me. I never would've done that. I don't know Caleb very well."

"You noticed how he was built."

"He's tall and muscular, like you. Women notice those sorts of things."

Curious about this Caleb character and the comparison she'd just made, he asked, "Are you interested in getting to know him better?"

"Oh, my goodness, no. The last I checked, he had eyes for my sister. But I don't think she's aware of his interest in her, and now that he's out of town, it doesn't matter anyway."

"It might when he gets back."

"For him, maybe. But for her? I doubt it. I can't see Donna dating a ranch hand. She's Ms. New York. Not that I have a right to criticize her."

"Why? Are you a fussy dater, too? Are you as picky about your men as your sister is about hers?"

She glanced away and started fidgeting. He'd obviously struck a chord. He should have left it alone, but he was too damned curious to drop it.

"Come on, Jenna. Fess up."

"There's nothing to fess."

He frowned, suddenly imagining her in a bad relationship. "Did someone hurt you? Did you get your heart broken?"

"Oh, no. It's nothing like that."

He felt immediately better. She'd been so kind to him, he didn't want to envision someone being unkind to her. "Then what is it?"

"I guess it won't matter if I tell you. But you're probably going to think it's dumb." She blew out a breath and continued, "I made a list of the qualities I want in a man, and I'm following it to the letter."

Well, then. That certainly wasn't what he expected. "I hope you find what you want."

"Me, too."

In the next curious instant, he wondered what sorts of qualities she was after. "Maybe you can show me the list sometime."

"I don't think that's a good idea."

"Why? Do you have sexual things on it?"

She straightened her spine, looking like a sweet little prude. "I can't believe you asked me that."

"Hey, you're the one who gave me a sexy name, remember?"

"I already explained that I didn't mean that literally."

"I know." He shot her a smile. "I was just teasing you."

"You have a wicked sense of humor."

He wondered if a sense of humor was on her list, but decided not to push the issue or tease her anymore about it.

Still, he couldn't get the list out of his mind. Sooner or later, he would probably ask her about it again.

He set Caleb's clothes aside and picked up the toiletry satchel. "Is there a shaving kit in here?"

"Truthfully, I've never taken inventory of what Donna puts in those, but she's a really thorough person, so I'm betting there is. I grabbed that from the supply room. I didn't even tell her that I was taking it."

"Let's see how thorough she is, shall we?"

"Sure. Let's see."

He opened the bag and started removing the items, placing them on the coffee table and reciting them, one by one. "Soap. Shampoo. Conditioner. Lotion. Toothpaste and mouthwash. Ah here we go. Shaving cream and disposable razors."

"Donna came through."

"Yes, she did." He reached into the satchel again. "There's a small box of some kind. It's wedged at the bottom." He dug it out of the bag and as soon as he held it up, he wanted to shove it back inside.

Condoms.

He looked at Jenna and she stared back at him. He couldn't think of a thing to say.

And apparently neither could she.

Jenna wanted to strangle herself for not checking out the items ahead of time. She wanted to strangle Donna, too, for being far more thorough than necessary.

Before the silence swallowed them alive, she managed a lame comment. "I guess my sister really did think of everything."

"She sure did." He seemed relieved that Jenna had broken the ice. He even smiled.

She was relieved that the moment had passed, too, but she struggled to summon a smile. Her heart was still beating with a quick cadence.

He put the condoms next to the razors. "Are you close?"

"What?"

"You and your sister?"

Funny he should ask. "No. I was just mentioning that to her this morning. How unalike we are. How we don't communicate all that well to each other."

"Did you discuss why?"

"No, but it's because of our family dynamics when we were growing up. Our parents got divorced when we were little, and we lived with our mom. Then she died when I was eight and Donna was nine."

"I'm sorry."

"It was ovarian cancer. I still miss her—Mom and I were close. Donna never bonded with her, or anyone, for that matter. But I think Donna wished she'd been closer to Mom. Sometimes, after Mom died, I used to catch her gazing at Mom's pictures in the most horribly sad way, but then Donna would look away, as if she didn't want me to know how badly she was hurting."

"What happened to you and Donna after your mom passed away?"

"We went to live with our dad. But he worked a lot, and we learned to fend for ourselves. I always wondered about my grandfather and his ranch. Secretly I wanted to meet him. But I knew Dad was estranged from his family, so I didn't talk to him about it. Dad isn't easy to talk to."

"You are."

She felt her cheeks go warm. "Really?"

"I'd tell you about myself if I knew who I was."

"The way I'm blabbing? Somehow, I doubt that."

"You're not blabbing. I asked you about your family and you're answering my questions."

In way too much detail, she thought. But it felt good

to get some of it off her chest. "The American dream was lost on my family."

"How common is that, really? How many people get to live that kind of life?"

"I don't know. But someday I want to create a family of my own, one that will be bonded and true to each other."

"Husband, kids, picket fence?"

She nodded. "I want a man who shares my love of the country. I feel blessed that I inherited part of this ranch. It's everything to me now, and I want it to be everything to my future husband."

"That stands to reason." He paused. "So, what was your grandfather like?"

"He went by the name of Tex. He was an ornery old guy, but charming, too. I regret not having the opportunity to know him better, but I'm grateful that he welcomed me into his life when he did." She thought about everything that had transpired recently. "Doc was his private physician. That's how he and Tammy met."

"And then they had dreams about each other that came true?" He glanced toward the bedroom. "If you don't mind me asking, what were those dreams?"

She'd avoided mentioning them earlier, but she supposed it didn't really matter since Doc and Tammy spoke openly about their experiences. "Tammy dreamed that she and Doc had a romantic evening in this cabin before it actually happened."

Clearly, J.D. wasn't impressed. "That's not very groundbreaking."

"Tammy worked hard to catch Doc's eye. In fact, I helped her with a makeover. She was a tomboy for most of her life and didn't know how to doll herself up."

"Doc doesn't seem like he's from around here."

"He isn't. He's originally from Philadelphia, and he came here to pay a debt to the man who put him through medical school, and that debt involved caring for our grandfather." She shifted on the sofa. "Doc was planning on leaving afterward and going back to his life in the city, then he fell in love with Tammy. He dreamed that they were happily married with three kids."

He frowned. "That's not a magic dream. They're not even married yet, and there aren't any kids."

"They're going to be married, and the kids will come later. Besides, they both dreamed about the same little dark-haired girl."

"Really?" He was obviously surprised.

"Yes, and someday that little girl is going to be born to them." Jenna was certain of it.

J.D. didn't respond, but she was glad that they'd had this discussion. Offering him a break, she said, "You should probably rest again."

"I won't be able to take another nap."

"You can watch TV."

"I don't like TV."

"So you do know something about yourself."

"I'm only saying that because when I turned on the TV in the hospital, it bored me."

"Then it probably bored you before you got amnesia, too."

"I don't know, but the man next to me sure liked to watch it."

"Yes, he did. I didn't care for his taste in shows." Especially the game show that reeked of her childhood. Jenna had always been sensitive about her youth, but even more so now that she was dealing with the Savannah Jeffries issue and her dad's part in it.

"What do you watch?" J.D. asked.

She pulled herself back into the conversation. "The news mostly. I like Animal Planet, too. Sometimes I watch romantic comedies."

"Is that what's called chick flicks?"

She nodded.

He got up and stood beside the living-room window. "So, how long have you had that list of yours?"

Dang. He was back to that. "Awhile."

"How long is awhile?"

"Since I was twenty-five, and I'm thirty now."

"Five years? That is awhile. Have you been refining it?"

"I added a few things about the ranch since I came here."

"About your future husband loving this place?"

"Yes." Restless, she reached for the clothes she'd loaned him. "But the list is mostly the same as it was five years ago. I knew what qualities I wanted in a man then, and I still want him to have those same qualities now."

"I couldn't begin to make a list. I don't know what I expect out of myself, let alone someone else."

"You'll know all about yourself once your memory comes back."

"I still can't imagine making a list."

"Then you're probably not a type-A personality like I am."

"I suppose not." He motioned to the clothes. "Is that part of your type-A nature?"

She glanced down. Apparently she'd been folding and refolding the same pair of jeans. "I'm just…"

"What?"

Nervous, she thought. But she said, "I'm just trying to help you get organized." She quickly folded each article of clothing, then went after the toiletries, dropping them back into the bag. She made sure the condoms went first, keeping them out of sight and out of mind. "I'll put all of this away for you."

"Sure. Okay. Thanks." He smiled a little. "I was going to leave everything there until I needed it."

So much for blocking the condoms from her mind. He wouldn't need those while he was staying at the Flying B, would he? Not unless he found a local girl to mess around with once he started feeling better.

Jenna frowned and headed for the bedroom.

He tagged along. "What's wrong?"

"Nothing."

"You seem flustered. If I'm too much work for you, just leave that stuff, Jenna. I'll take care of it."

"I'm not flustered." She just didn't like envisioning him with another woman.

As opposed to him being with her? She reprimanded herself. She shouldn't be entertaining those sorts of thoughts. J.D. could have sex with whoever met his fancy.

Trouble was, he met the physical requirements on her list. Of course she knew that being sexually attracted to someone wasn't enough to sustain a relationship. Every piece of the puzzle had to fit.

While she put his borrowed clothes in the dresser, he sat on the edge of the bed.

"You should stay in this cabin after I'm gone," he said.

"Why?"

"So you can sleep here." He patted the bed.

Her pulse went haywire. "I already told you there's nothing I need to dream about."

"I was talking about the comfort factor."

"I have a comfortable bed in my room."

"Do you have an old feather mattress?"

"No."

"Then I'll bet it doesn't compare. I sank right into this bed. It's pretty darn amazing."

She glanced away. "I'm glad you like it."

"It's interesting that you don't think you have anything to dream about."

She turned to look at him again. "What do you mean?"

"Seems to me that you'd want to dream about the man you're hoping to marry."

"I don't need to see him in a dream. I'll know who he is when I meet him in person."

"You'll recognize him from the list? That must be some list."

"It is to me. But most people probably wouldn't think much of it."

"Where do you keep it?"

"I have a file on my computer. But I keep a copy in my purse, too."

"You carry it around?" He flashed his lopsided grin. "That's over the top."

His cavalier attitude annoyed her. "Keeping it close at hand helps me to stay focused."

"So you can checkmark it when you're on a date?"

His grin got even more crooked. "I feel sorry for the poor saps who take you out, having to live up to whatever your expectations are."

"Your sense of humor is wearing thin, J.D."

"Sorry. It's just that I've never met anyone like you before."

"How would you know if you've ever met anyone like me?"

"I wouldn't, I guess. But logic tells me that you're one of a kind."

"You think I'm weird." She tromped into the bathroom to put his toiletries away.

Soon she felt his presence behind her. She sensed that he was looming in the doorway, watching her. She ignored him. The condoms were the last items she put away. She placed them in the cabinet under the sink, stood up and turned in his direction.

He said, "I don't think you're weird. I think you're sweet and beautiful and unique."

He was looking at her with tenderness in his eyes, and now she longed to reach out and hold him. "Thank you. That was a nice thing to say."

"I meant every word."

The bathroom was small already, and now the walls were closing in.

"I should get going," she said.

"You don't have to leave yet."

She glanced at her watch. "It's getting late."

"But I want you to stay." He didn't move away from the doorway, trapping her where she was.

J.D. scrambled for an excuse to keep her there. "I need you to help me put the groceries away."

"You already put them away."

"I just put the bags in the fridge. I didn't unload them."

"Oh, my goodness. Really? There was frozen food in those. And canned goods and…" She shook her head. "You should have unpacked them."

"So help me do it now."

She made a *tsk-tsk* sound. "Who doesn't look in a grocery bag to see what's in it?"

He smiled. "A guy recovering from a concussion?"

She returned his smile, and he realized he'd just charmed her. It made him feel good inside, but a bit anxious, too. He shouldn't be asking her to spend more time with him.

"Come on," she said. "Let's put the food away properly."

He cleared the doorway, allowing her to pass by him. As her body breezed by his, he got a zipper-tugging sensation. He took a rough breath and followed her to the kitchen. While he was walking behind her, he checked her out. She was lean and gently toned. Had he always been partial to small-framed girls?

She made a beeline for the fridge and removed the bags. Together, they unloaded them. She'd gotten him a variety of stuff to choose from: frozen pizza, fresh fruit, ready-made salads, boxed macaroni and cheese, sandwich fixings, canned chili, soup and crackers, pudding cups, cereal and milk.

Meals designed for a bachelor, he thought. "Thank you again for everything you've been doing for me. I really do intend to repay you."

"All I want is for you to get better," she said, repeating what she'd told him earlier. "That will be payment enough."

"I'm glad you didn't get anything that requires cooking skills. I don't think I'd be very good in that regard."

"We have that in common."

He nodded. She'd already mentioned that she wasn't much of a cook.

After they completed their task, he said, "Will you sit outside with me before you go?" He was still looking for excuses to keep her there, and since the cabin was equipped with a quaint little porch, it provided a cozy atmosphere. "We can have some pudding."

She accepted the invitation, and they settled into mismatched chairs. The air was rife with something sweet. Honeysuckle, maybe. Foliage grew along the sides of the building.

As he spooned into his dessert, he looked at Jenna, impressed with how beautifully she fit into the environment. Her hair caught the setting sun, making it look even blonder. He couldn't explain why her hair was a source of fascination. Was it because his was so dark? His skin was a lot darker than hers, too.

"I wish I could cook," she said, her mind obviously back in the kitchen.

"You could learn, couldn't you?"

"I don't know. Every time I try to make something, it tastes awful. Maybe I'll ask Tammy if she can give me some pointers."

"The way you gave her pointers about dolling herself up?"

Jenna smiled. "It might be a good trade."

"Sounds like it to me." He studied her again. She certainly knew how to make herself look pretty. Whatever she was wearing on her lips created a warm, kissable effect. "You can use me as a guinea pig if you want."

"For my cooking?"

Or kissing, he thought. "Yes, cooking."

"You're already suffering from a head injury. I don't want to poison you, too."

"I'm sure I'd survive it."

"I'd rather not take the chance."

"I probably won't be here long enough anyway." No poison food. No soft, sweet, poison kisses, either. He needed to stop thinking about how alluring she was.

"Do you like the pudding?" she asked.

He glanced at his cup. He'd only taken a few bites. He'd been too busy admiring her. "Yes, it's good."

"Butterscotch is my favorite."

He noticed that she'd barely made a dent in hers, either. "You're not gobbling it up very quickly."

"I'm savoring it."

"So am I," he lied, when in fact, he'd been savoring her.

"This is nice, sitting out here with you."

"Thanks. I think so, too." He couldn't envision anything nicer. Well, actually he could, but he'd warned himself not to obsess about kissing her. "We're becoming friends."

Friends and only friends, he reiterated.

While a soft Texas breeze blew, he asked, "What's the name of this town?"

"Buckshot Hills. I'm surprised no one told you before now."

"It must have slipped their minds."

"It slipped mine. I wonder how long it will take for Deputy Tobbs to start questioning the locals about you."

"Soon, I hope."

"Once you're feeling better, I can take you on a tour of the Flying B and introduce you to the people who work here, like Deputy Tobbs suggested."

"Wouldn't it be ironic if I was on my way to visit someone at the Flying B when I got hurt?"

"It would certainly solve the mystery, and quickly, too."

There was a mixed-up part of him that wished he'd been on his way to visit her, that she'd been his agenda. No matter how hard he tried, he couldn't seem to control his attraction to her. He even worried that he might have an intimate dream about her tonight, with or without a so-called magic bed.

After they finished their pudding, she said, "I really should go now."

He didn't try to stop her. It was better to have some distance between them.

She left, and he watched her go.

About an hour later, someone rapped at the door, and he jumped up to answer it, wondering if she'd returned.

But it was Doc, with his medical bag.

The other man said, "Jenna told me that she put you up in this cabin. How do you like it?"

"It's fine. But I don't believe that the bed is magical. I know you do, though."

"I'm a man of science, but I've learned that sometimes logic doesn't apply."

J.D. didn't respond, and the subject was dropped. Regardless, the feeling remained. He was still concerned that he might have a sensual dream.

Doc examined him and recommended more bed rest.

J.D. followed orders and went to sleep early that night. He didn't dream about Jenna.

Much to his shock, he dreamed about himself, with an emotion-packed glimpse of who he was as a child.

Chapter Four

Jenna looked across the table at Donna. They were having breakfast together again, and today Donna was paging through wallpaper samples that were stacked beside her.

"We really should stop meeting like this," Jenna said.

Her sister glanced up and rolled her eyes. But she smiled, too, lightening the moment.

After their mom died, they rarely shared a meal. They would just grab their food and go. Actually, they hadn't dined together all that much when Mom had been around, either. She'd been depressed over the divorce, then she'd gotten sick.

"Our childhoods sucked," Jenna said, thinking out loud.

Donna crinkled her face. "This isn't a discussion we should be having."

"Why not?"

"Because sitting around wallowing in the past isn't going to change anything."

"I wasn't wallowing." She was trying to have a meaningful conversation. "It wouldn't hurt to talk things through once in a while."

"I don't see the point in crying over spilt milk. We need to focus on the B and B and making it a success."

"That's what we've been doing."

"Then let's not lose sight of it."

Jenna considered her sister's determination. A failed business venture had put a dent in Donna's bankbook, damaging her self-esteem and putting her glamorous life at risk. The B and B was her chance to make up for it.

Donna lifted a paisley-printed swatch. "What do you think of this for the bedroom that overlooks the garden?"

"What garden?"

"The one I'm designing with the landscaper. I told you about it before."

"No, you didn't."

"Oh, I'm sorry. I thought I did. It's going to have a redwood gazebo and a boatload of flowering perennials. Daisies in the summer, Texas bluebonnets in the spring. It'll be a perfect spot for weddings and special events."

"It sounds beautiful, and I think the wallpaper is pretty, too."

"I don't know." Donna gave the swatch a critical eye. "Maybe I should use a Western pattern. My goal is to create an idyllic atmosphere but without infringing on the natural environment."

"You're doing a great job so far."

"Thank you."

"I've always admired your sense of style." Jenna hadn't been born with a gift of flair, not like her sister. "I learned how to put myself together from watching you."

"Really?" Donna seemed surprised, maybe even a little embarrassed by the praise. "Well, you know what? You did a spectacular job of helping Tammy with her makeover. She looks like a million now."

"It was fun, and she nabbed the prize, too."

"The Prince Charming doctor? You'd never catch me playing the role of Cinderella."

For a moment, Jenna was tempted to tell Donna about Caleb's interest in her, but she figured it was pointless since it wouldn't go anywhere, anyway. She said instead, "I gave J.D. one of the toiletry satchels you created for our guests."

"Who's J.D.?"

"The man with amnesia. That's what we're calling him until we know his real name. It's the initials for John Doe. I offered to let him stay at the ranch until his memory returns or until the police uncover his identity."

"I wonder which will come first."

"I don't know. I put him in the dream cabin."

"Did he like the toiletries? I labored over what brand of shampoo and conditioner to order."

"I'm sure the shampoo and conditioner will be just fine, when he's able to use them. For now, he isn't supposed to get his stitches wet." But that was the least of Jenna's concern. "Why did you include condoms in those bags?"

"Because other top-notch establishments provide prophylactics to their guests. Actually, I was thinking that I should use little baskets to display everything instead of the satchels. What do you think?"

"Baskets would definitely be better. No surprises. I nearly died when J.D. pulled the condoms out of that bag."

Donna furrowed her delicately arched brows. "Don't tell me you have a crush on him."

"What?"

"Why else would you want to die over a box of condoms?"

"Because I barely know him."

"Are you sure that's all it is?"

"Yes."

"Good. Because Flying B romances are chock-full of trouble."

"That isn't a very nice thing to say about Tammy and Doc."

"I wasn't talking about them. It's nice that Tammy is walking around all shiny and new."

"So, you were talking about Savannah Jeffries? Maybe it's time for us to have a discussion about her."

"I'd rather not." Although the detachment in Donna's voice was evident, so was the vulnerability. "Savannah Jeffries has nothing to do with our future."

Jenna wasn't so sure about that. Already Savannah was affecting them. "We can't ignore it forever. We're going to have to vote on the P.I. issue."

"Not at the moment, we don't."

True. The rest of the family had to decide, as well— the rest of them being Tammy and her brothers, Aidan and Nathan.

The fathers were being excluded from the vote, mostly because Jenna and Donna didn't want their dad to have a say in the mess he'd made. As for Uncle William, Tammy said that he preferred to be left out of it anyway, as he just wanted the whole thing to disappear. *The way Savannah had disappeared,* Jenna thought.

Suddenly her cell phone rang. She glanced at the screen and saw the landline number from the dream cabin. She walked away from the table and answered it.

"J.D.?" she said.

"I hope I'm not disturbing you."

"No, not at all. How are you feeling?"

"Truthfully? I'm overwhelmed. The bed worked, Jenna. I dreamed about myself last night. A memory dream. Do you want to come by and I'll tell you about it?"

Her heart struck her chest. "Yes, of course. I'm on my way."

The call ended, and she approached table. "I have to go," she told Donna.

Her sister turned in her chair. "Is everything all right?"

"Yes." At least she hoped it was. J.D. didn't say if his dream was good or bad. *Overwhelmed* could apply to either.

She left the house and climbed in her truck. The cabin was within walking distance, but only on a leisure day. She wanted to hurry up and get there.

She arrived within a matter of minutes, and he was waiting for her on the porch.

She ascended the steps and they stood face-to-face. He was clean shaven, and without the stubble, his strong-boned features were even more pronounced.

He was wearing one of Caleb's shirts, but he'd left it unbuttoned. The jeans were Caleb's, too, and they fit him a little snugger than his own. She assumed that he had a pair of the new boxers on underneath.

"Do you want to talk out here or go inside?" he asked.

"It's up to you." Where they conversed didn't matter. She was distracted by him: his abs, his navel, the frayed waistband of his borrowed jeans. Even his bare feet seemed sexy.

He said, "Let's stay out here."

Normally the outdoors soothed her. But being around J.D. was turning her into a jumble of hormones. She'd lied to Donna about not having a crush on him.

Instead of taking a chair, he sat on the porch steps. She had no choice but to sit beside him, far closer than a chair would've allowed.

"Was it a good dream?" she asked quickly.

"Yes, but it was troubling, too. I saw myself as a boy. I was about ten. I was in a barn, grooming a sorrel mare. I grew up around horses, Jenna. I could feel it during the dream."

"Why is that troubling?" She thought it was wonderful. She'd pegged him as a cowboy from the beginning.

"I was the only person in the dream. I didn't get a feeling about my family. For all I know, I could have been a foster kid who was too old to get adopted."

That struck her as an odd thing for him to say. Was it a memory struggling to surface? "Were you sad in the dream?"

"No. But I was with the mare, and I felt a connection to her. She made me happy."

Horses always made Jenna happy, too, but they gave a lot of people joy. His bond with the mare didn't prove or disprove what type of childhood he'd had. His foster care/adoption comment was too specific to ignore, though. "Maybe the dream will continue on another night."

"Maybe."

She studied his chiseled profile. "What did you look like as a ten-year-old?"

"Why does that matter?"

"I just want to know." To see him through his own eyes.

"I was on the small side, a skinny kid, and my hair was sort of longish. A little messy, I suppose." He shrugged, but he smiled, too. "I was wearing a straw cowboy hat, and I had sugar cubes in my shirt pocket for the mare."

She smiled, as well. She liked envisioning him as a youth and she liked the boyishness that had come over him now. He seemed wistful. If he hadn't made the foster-child remark, she would've assumed that he'd had a solid upbringing. But he had made the remark, and it weighed heavily on her mind.

"Tell me more about the dream," she said. "Were you in Texas? Is that where you grew up?"

"I don't know. I didn't get a sense of the location."

"What was the barn like?"

"I couldn't tell how big it was, but it was well maintained."

"Did you get a sense of how long you'd lived there?"

"No."

"But you sensed that you'd been raised in an equine environment?"

"Yes."

"So if you were a foster child, then all of the homes

you'd been placed in had horses? How likely do you think that is?"

"I have no idea." He changed the subject. "So, why don't you tell me about the horses on the Flying B?"

"We have plenty of great trail horses that Tex used to favor and that anyone on the ranch can use at their leisure, but I'm still acquiring school horses."

"For your riding instruction?"

She nodded. "They have to be able to accommodate any level of rider. I'll need a string of them for group lessons, but I'm being extremely cautious, hand-selecting each one. I have two wonderful geldings, so far."

"Will you take me to see them?"

"Today?"

"Yes, now. Today. I want to know how being around horses makes me feel in person. You can introduce me to the employees on the ranch, too, and see if any of them recognize me."

"I think I better check with Doc before I take you on a tour. You've only been out of the hospital for a day."

"I feel fine."

"I still think I should talk to him." She removed her phone from her purse and called Doc, but she got his answering service. "He's supposed to call me back."

"When?"

"As soon as he's able."

J.D. stood up. "I'm going to get ready."

He went into the cabin and came back, carrying his socks and boots. Jenna couldn't blame him for being anxious, but what if he was jumping the gun?

"Doc might not think you're ready for an outing," she said.

"He will if you tell him about my dream. Besides, I'll go stir-crazy just sitting around here."

After his boots were in place, he buttoned his shirt and tucked it into his pants.

"I forgot my belt." Off he went to retrieve it.

She took a moment to breathe, as deeply as she could. Watching him get dressed was making her warm and tingly.

He returned with the belt halfway threaded through his belt loops. She should've turned away, but like the smitten female she was fast becoming, she trained her gaze on his every move.

This was crazy. Now she felt as if she had a concussion, and she hadn't even taken a hit to the head. Not literally, anyway. Figuratively, she'd been struck and struck hard.

Determined to keep her wits, she thought about her list. Aside from his physical attributes and his newly discovered connection to horses, he didn't meet her requirements. First and foremost, the man she chose had to be as marriage-minded as she was, and J.D. didn't seem like the husband type. Nor was she foolish enough to believe that he was going to dream himself into that role.

He sat beside her, pulling her out of analytical mode and back into a heap of emotion. His nearness caused a chemical reaction.

Fire in her veins. Pheromones shooting from her pores.

Before the silence grew unbearable, she said, "If you were raised around horses, then I'll bet you're a skilled rider."

He shot her a half-cocked grin. "Give me a bucking bronc to ride and we'll see."

She laughed, albeit nervously. She hadn't recovered from his nearness. "All I need is for you to get tossed on your head. Doc would accuse me of trying to kill his patient."

Finally the doctor in question called, and Jenna spoke with him.

Afterward, she told J.D., "He said it was fine, as long as you don't stay too long or wear yourself out."

"I knew he would agree." He reached over to give her a hand up.

Being touched by him didn't help her condition. She was still fighting fire, pheromones and everything else that had gone wrong with her.

"Are we going to walk?" he asked.

"I think it would be better to take the truck."

He glanced out in the distance. "How far is it?"

"Not that far. But too far for a man with a head injury," she amended. "Doc said not to tax your energy."

"Did he specifically say that I shouldn't walk?"

"No, but I'm saying it." For the second time that day, she avoided a leisurely stroll.

After they got in the truck, he turned toward her. "Thanks, Jenna."

"For what?"

"Putting up with me. I know I'm taking up a lot of your time."

"It's okay. I want to help you through this." And once he was completely well, she could try to resume some order in her life. "Look at the progress you've made already."

"Because of you and your family. You really should

stay in the cabin after I'm gone, even if it's just for one night."

"The bed in my room is fine."

"The bed in your room doesn't induce dreams."

She repeated what she'd told him before. "I don't need to rely on magic. Things will happen for me when they're meant to."

"But you seem tense."

She started the engine and headed toward the stables. "There's a lot going on in my world."

"Like the Savannah Jeffries issue?"

"Yes."

"If you need a sounding board, I'll lend you my ear."

"I tried to talk to my sister about it this morning."

"But she didn't want to discuss it?"

"No."

"I'm here, if you need me," he reiterated.

There was a part of her that wanted to tell him the whole sordid story, to lean on his shoulder and let him wrap her in comfort. But relying on him wasn't the answer, especially with her troubled attraction to him.

She parked in front of the stables and introduced him to the ranch hands who were nearby. None of them recognized him. Neither did Hugh, the loyal old foreman who'd snagged Caleb's clothes. But she didn't expect Hugh to recognize him, especially since she'd already described J.D. to him.

"You can meet everyone else on another day," she told J.D.

He agreed, and she took him to the barn that housed the school horses.

"This is Pedro's Pride," she said as a tobiano paint

poked his head out to greet them. She opened the gate and they went into his stall. "But I just call him Pedro."

J.D. approached the horse, and it was love at first sight. Man and beast connected instantly. Jenna stood back and marveled at the exchange.

"He's big and flashy," J.D. said, "But he has manners, too."

As he roamed his hands along the gelding's sturdy frame, the horse stood patiently. Jenna wasn't quite so calm. Seeing J.D. this way heightened her feelings for him.

He said, "If Pedro carries a rider the way you say he does, then you found a gem."

"You look as if you found a gem, too. In yourself," she clarified. "I can tell that you're in your element."

"I am. It feels right." He tapped a hand to his chest. "Here, where it counts."

In his heart, she thought. "That's how I feel every time I come out here."

"You're lucky that this is your life's work."

"It's probably yours, too. You just can't remember the who, what and where."

He remained next to the gelding. "How long will Caleb be out of town?"

"I think he's scheduled to come back next month. Why?"

"If you need someone to fill in for him until he gets back, maybe you can hire me. Then I can repay your kindness by working it off."

Yesterday, he'd been unable to acknowledge that he might be a cowboy, and today he was offering to be a ranch hand. But given the circumstances, his offer made sense. "I'll have to talk to Hugh about it, and to Doc, too, of course. You can't start working until he gives you a clean bill of health." She added, "And you'll get the same wages as everyone else. Repaying my kindness doesn't mean that you'll be working for free."

"I won't let you, Hugh or Doc down. I'll do a good job."

"I'm sure you will." But it was only temporary, she reminded herself.

J.D. wasn't going to be part of the Flying B forever.

J.D. glanced at Pedro, then at Jenna. He felt perfectly at ease around the horse. But around the woman? Not so much. The zip-zing between them jarred his senses.

He wanted to do right by her, to work at the ranch and make himself useful. But somewhere in the pit of his stomach, he wanted to run to the nearest bus stop and leave Buckshot Hills, Texas, far, far behind.

He'd seen the way she'd looked at him when he'd gotten halfway dressed in front of her. True, he'd been antsy about meeting her horses, but he shouldn't have buttoned his shirt or zipped his jeans in her presence, especially since it had been a fantasy leftover from the hospital.

"How are you feeling?" she asked.

He blinked. "What?"

"I want to be sure you're feeling well enough to continue."

"I'm doing fine." Except for his bad-to-the-bone hunger for her.

"Then let's go to the next stall."

They proceeded, and she introduced him to Duke, her other school horse, whose original owner, a lover of old Westerns, had given him the same nickname as

John Wayne. He was a friendly sorrel with a blaze and three white socks. J.D. approached the gelding, anxious to get close to him.

"He resembles the mare in my dream. His markings are similar." And it made J.D. feel like the boy he once was. "If I had a sugar cube, I'd give him one."

"You can spoil him next time. And Pedro, too."

"I wish I could ride him."

"Next time," she said again.

"How old were you when you started riding?" he asked.

"Ten."

"The same age I was in my dream."

She nodded. "I was one of those kids that collected horsey stuff—pictures, books, toys, stuffed animals—but other than a few pony rides, I wasn't around them. Then, two years after Mom died, I asked Dad if I could take riding lessons. He agreed, but he didn't take an active part in it. He didn't drive me back and forth or watch me during my lessons. He hired a babysitter for that, and once I got old enough to go on my own, I hung out there all the time, before and after school, on weekends, in the summer. It was a magnificent equestrian center. My home away from home."

"So, what did you look like when you were ten?" he asked, interested to know the same thing about her that she'd wanted to know about him.

She smiled. "I was a skinny kid with longish hair."

He smiled, too. She'd stolen his line. "Did you favor straw hats?"

"Are you kidding? I still do."

"I haven't seen you in a hat yet."

"You will. Speaking of which, you're going to need

one once you start working here. I can give you one that belonged to my grandfather."

"You don't have to do that."

"Tex wouldn't have minded. He probably would have given you one himself. I think your dream would have fascinated him."

He thought about his unknown family. "Do you think I was a foster kid?"

"I don't know. But your comment about possibly being too old to be adopted gave me pause."

It gave him pause, too. "Most people want babies or toddlers, not older kids." He frowned. "Don't they?"

"I don't know anything about adoption, J.D."

He searched her gaze. "Would you ever consider raising someone else's child as your own?"

"Truthfully, I've never really thought about it before. But I love children, so if it was something my husband wanted to do, I would certainly consider it. What about you?"

"Me?" He took a cautionary step back. "I don't think I'd make a very good dad, adoptive or otherwise. I'd have enough trouble dealing with myself, let alone being a parent."

"My future husband is going to be father material. That's one of the most important qualities on my list. I want him to bring our children presents, even when it isn't their birthdays. I want him to help me read to them at night. I even want him to dress up as Santa Claus and sneak past the tree on Christmas Eve."

Surprised that she referred to the list she'd been protecting, he said, "I wouldn't be able to do any of that." Even now, he felt as if he were on the brink of a panic attack. "Marriage, babies, birthdays, Christmas."

"I wasn't implying that you should."

"Neither was I." He fought the panic, forcing his lungs to expand. "I was just making conversation."

"About how different we are? I already figured that out."

Of course she did, he thought. She analyzed the men she was attracted to. She weighed them against her list.

She said, "After your identity is restored, you can return to whatever type of lifestyle suits you."

He nodded, knowing that was exactly what he would do. Nonetheless, it didn't give him comfort. The fact that Jenna found him lacking made him ache inside.

An ache he couldn't begin to understand.

Chapter Five

A week passed without J.D. having any more dreams and without the police uncovering any information about him. But at least Doc said that he was well enough to work. And ride, which he'd done, but only minimally. He hadn't had the opportunity to spend a lot of time in the saddle yet. Mostly his work entailed maintenance in and around the barn.

As for Jenna, his hunger for her was getting worse. In spite of the fact that they were completely wrong for each other, he felt like a thunderstruck kid.

Today he was mucking out stalls, and she was reorganizing the tack room. Every so often, as he moved about the barn, he would catch sight of her in the tack room doorway, and his heart would dive straight to his stomach.

"J.D.?" a male voice said, drawing his attention.

He turned to see Manny, another ranch hand, coming toward him. By now, J.D. had met all of the other employees on the Flying B., including the household staff. Manny, he'd learned, had a thing for one of the maids, a girl he talked incessantly about. J.D., however, hadn't said a word about his forbidden interest in Jenna.

Manny flashed a youthful grin. He was all of twenty-two, with curly brown hair and a happy-go-lucky personality. J.D. wished he knew how to feel that way, but the more time that passed, the more he sensed that his emotions had been screwed up long before Jenna had found him and brought him here.

Manny said, "A group of us are getting together at Lucy's tonight. You ought to join us, J.D. It might do you some good to get out."

"Who's Lucy?"

"It's a place, not a person. Lone Star Lucy's. The local honky-tonk. So, do you want to go?"

"Sure, okay. Thanks." He didn't have anything else to do.

Manny grinned again. "Some of the household staff is going, too."

J.D. cracked a smile. The other man's infectious energy seemed to demand it. "I take it that means the gal you're hot for will be there?"

"Heck, yeah. And I'm going to stick to her like glue. You just watch me."

"I don't doubt that you will." J.D. couldn't seem to stop from asking, "Are any of the Byrds going?" He wanted Jenna to be there. He wanted to see her as badly as Manny wanted to see the maid.

"No."

"Why not?"

"Nobody thought to invite them, I guess. We haven't mingled with them outside the ranch."

"Then maybe it's time."

"You can ask them to come, if you want. I wouldn't count on the prissy one showing up, though. She wouldn't fit in." Manny chuckled. "What's her name? Dana?"

"Donna. I met her briefly, a few days ago." A quick introduction when Jenna had taken him inside to meet the household staff. "She doesn't seem easy to get to know." Which had given him a clearer understanding of the lack of closeness between the sisters.

"I've seen her walking around, dodging manure and sniffling from the hay. I'm surprised she's lasted as long as she has."

"I'll invite all of the Byrds to keep from being rude." And to keep it from seeming as if he only had Jenna in mind. "It would be nice to see Doc and Tammy out on the town."

"Yeah, Tammy is country folk, and Doc is getting there, too. Make sure you don't forget about Jenna, not after everything she's done for you. I think you should buy her a drink."

"I agree. I'll do that, if she accepts the invite." He tried to seem casual. "She told me that she likes to dance so maybe I'll two-step with her, too, if I can keep up." He still wasn't sure what kind of dancer he was, but he was willing to find out if it meant having Jenna as his partner.

"Great. Sounds like a party to me. I can give you a ride. Let's say, about eight? I'll swing by your cabin."

"All right. See you then."

Manny returned to work, and J.D. put down his rake

and walked over to where Jenna was. He entered the tack room, and she looked up from the bridles she was hanging on wooden pegs.

He got right to the point. "Manny asked me to join him and some of the others at Lucy's tonight. It would be nice if you, Tammy, Doc and Donna wanted to meet us there."

"Donna would never go to Lucy's."

"Yeah, that's what Manny figured. How about you? Do you want to go?"

"I don't know if it's the right place for me, either. From what I've heard, it caters to a wild crowd."

Hoping to thwart her concern, he said, "I'll protect you from the crazies."

"You will, huh?" She laughed a little. "And who's going to protect me from you?"

"If Doc and Tammy go, Doc can keep me in line. He can tranquilize me if I get too rowdy."

She laughed again. "Then I'll make sure they come along."

Damn, but he liked her. "I thought maybe you and I could dance. Or I'd like to give it a try anyway."

"That sounds nice."

"We're leaving around eight. You can head over about the same time if you want."

"I'll do my best."

Before he overstepped his bounds, he said, "I should get back to work now."

"Me, too." She made a show of jangling the bridles in her hand.

"Bye, Jenna."

"Bye."

He walked away, dreading the day he had to say

goodbye to her for real. But at least for now, he had the chance to hold her while they danced.

Jenna walked into Lone Star Lucy's, where scores of people gathered. Doc and Tammy couldn't make it, so she'd ventured out on her own—clearly a stupid thing to do, especially at a bar like this.

She didn't have a clue where J.D. or the Flying B employees were. Everyone looked alike in the dimly lit, sawdust-on-the-floor, tables-crammed-too-close-together environment. Most of the men were bold and flirtatious, with their hats dipped low and their beer bottles held high, and most of the women wore their makeup too heavy, their hair too big and their jeans too tight.

As she made her way farther into the room, she noticed the dance floor. A digital jukebox provided the music. Way in the back, she caught a glimpse of pool tables.

J.D. had said that he would protect her from the crazies, but already she was getting hit on.

A cowboy with slurred speech leaned over his chair and grabbed her shirtsleeve. "Where are you going in such a hurry?"

She tugged her arm away. "I'm looking for someone."

"I can be your someone," he replied.

It is time to leave, she thought. She turned around and ran smack-dab into J.D. He stood there, like a wall of muscle.

"Is that guy bothering you?" he asked.

Her pulse went pitter-pat. "He was, but he isn't anymore."

Slurred Speech had gone back to his beer.

"Where's Doc and Tammy?" J.D. asked.

"They had other plans."

"You should have let me know you were alone. You could have ridden with us."

"You and Manny?"

"And some of the other guys."

"A truckload of testosterone? I don't know about that."

"We would have made room for you, and you could have sat up front with me."

She envisioned herself squeezed in the middle, practically sharing the same seat with J.D. "Taking my own truck was fine."

"I'm just happy you're here. You look damn fine, Jenna."

"Thank you." Her boot-cut jeans were as tight as every other cowgirl's in the place. She'd gone easy on the makeup, though, aside from the crimson lipstick that matched her fancy silk blouse. She hadn't overdone her hair, either. She wore it loose and soft.

He kept looking at her with appreciation in his eyes, and his dark gaze whipped her into a girlish flutter. She'd wanted to impress him, and she had.

"Come on," he said. "I'll take you to our table."

He put his hand lightly on the small of her back, and as they weaved their way around other patrons, he never broke contact. His gentle touch heightened her girlish reaction to him.

He motioned with his free hand. "Over there."

She saw the Flying B group, with Manny smiling big and bright amongst his peers.

There were nine people in all, including her and J.D.

He'd saved a seat for her. He'd saved seats for Doc and Tammy, too. But as soon as it became apparent that they weren't being used, they were quickly snatched up by people at another table.

Jenna was greeted by the Flying B employees. The other women in attendance were part-timers from the housekeeping staff. Their names were Celia, Joy and Maria, and they looked a lot different here than they did at work. Celia's boobs were busting out of her top, Joy had eyeliner out to there and Maria's dress hugged her curvaceous hips. They smelled of the same flowery perfume, too, a telltale sign that they'd gotten ready together, sharing a bottle of whatever it was. Overall they seemed like nice girls who'd gone into Lucy's mode for the night.

J.D. turned to Jenna. "Would you like a drink? I'm buying."

"You shouldn't spend your money on me." She knew he'd gotten an advance on his pay, but it wasn't much.

"Are you kidding? I owe you more than a drink."

She offered a smile. "You owe me a dance, too."

His smile matched hers. "First a drink."

She considered white wine, but changed her mind. "I'll take a longneck." She motioned to his bottle. "The same kind you're having."

"I'll get it from the bar. It'll take the waitress forever to work her way over here." Before he left, he finished his beer, which apparently had been almost gone. One last swallow.

He stood up, and she watched him walk away. He had an awfully cute butt. But before someone caught her admiring his backside, she turned her attention to the people she was with and noticed that Manny had eyes for Maria. She seemed flattered by the attention, leaning toward him when he talked and laughing at silly things he said. Now she understood why Manny had orchestrated this get-together. He wanted to make something happen with Maria.

J.D. returned with Jenna's beer. She thanked him and noticed that he'd gotten himself another one, too.

She hoped that he didn't overindulge. It was bad enough that she'd assumed he was drunk when she'd first seen him, lest it come true this evening. She still knew very little about J.D and his habits. Of course he knew little about himself, too. Each day was a new exploration.

Earlier, he'd joked about having Doc tranquilize him, and she'd laughed at the time. But it wouldn't be funny if he got carried away.

Luckily, he didn't. He sipped his second drink slowly.

"We should share a toast," he said.

"To what?"

"Us spending the night together."

She blinked at him. She also felt her skin flush. Suddenly, she was racked with heat. Her nipples shot out like bullets against her bra, too. "We're not spending the night together."

"That isn't what I said."

"Yes, it is."

"No, it isn't," he countered. "I said that we were spending the night *out* together."

"You left off the *out* part."

"I did? Are you sure?"

She nodded. She knew the difference.

"It's noisy in here. Maybe you misheard me."

"You goofed up, J.D." He'd made a Freudian slip or whatever mistakes like that were called.

"I'm sorry. I didn't realize..." He fidgeted with his beer.

Now she wished that she would have kept quiet. "I'm sorry, too. I shouldn't have pointed it out."

The subject was dropped, but that didn't ease the moment.

Just when she thought it couldn't get any worse, Manny glanced across the table and said, "When are you guys going to dance?"

"In a while," J.D. responded.

"You don't look like you're having a very good time." Manny cocked his head. "Either of you."

Jenna piped up. "We're just being quiet while we finish our drinks."

"Liquid courage," J.D. said. "I'll probably suck out there."

Manny replied, "You should have done a test run at the ranch and danced around the cabin."

J.D. made a face. "Now how stupid would I have looked?"

"Pretty dang dumb." The other man grinned. "But at least you would've known if you were any good."

"I don't think it would have been the same without a partner. I won't know until I try it for real."

"We're going to dance later, too," Manny said, and moved closer to Maria. "We're waiting for the songs we picked to play."

He turned back to the rest of the group, leaving J.D. and Jenna to their silent agony. Heaven help her, but she wanted to spend the night with him, to make love, to sleep beside him in the dream cabin. But she knew that being with him would create emotional havoc. Dallying with a man who was destined to disappear from her life wasn't part of her get-married-and-have-babies plan.

"Should we pick some songs, too?" he asked. "It might help us relax."

She appreciated his attempt to make things better. "Sure. Let's give it a try."

He stood up, and like a knight in shining armor, he pulled back her chair. "Chivalry" was one of the husband-requirements on her list. She frowned to herself. As always, her list was tucked away in her purse.

They proceeded to the digital jukebox and waited for the people in front of them to make their selections.

When their turn arrived, he said, "I like the old-style jukes better."

"Me, too. But we live in a digital world now."

"Some things should remain the same."

Like chivalrous men, she thought, fighting another frown. Tonight, of all nights, she shouldn't be referring to her list, especially since J.D wasn't in the running.

He scanned the songs. "The jukebox might be new, but at least the music is classic country."

She stood beside him. "Oh, I love this song." She gestured to "Breathe" by Faith Hill.

"That's a romantic one."

"I wasn't suggesting that we dance to it. I was just saying that it's a favorite of mine."

"Do you like this one, too?" He pointed to Faith's duet with Tim McGraw called "Let's Make Love."

"Now you're being smart." And making a naughty joke about his Freudian slip. "You and that wicked sense of humor of yours."

He flashed a dastardly smile. "Are you brave enough to dance to it with me?"

Was she?

"Are you?" he asked again.

Why not? she thought. At this point, it seemed better to acknowledge their chemistry than try to avoid it. "Go ahead and push the button. But we'll probably smolder on the dance floor and make everyone jealous."

"If I don't step all over your feet."

"That would certainly ruin the ambience."

"I can't guarantee it won't happen." He chose the song. "Any more?"

"I think one is enough, considering. Don't you?"

"Yeah. We probably shouldn't bite off more than we can chew." They stepped away from the jukebox and he said, "Did you know that Manny has a thing for Maria?"

She looked across the room and toward their table. "Yes, I noticed that he's into her. She seems to like him, too. They'll probably start dating after tonight."

"That will make Manny happy. Who knows how long it will last, though?"

"They're young. They have lots of time to find who they're meant to be with."

"Do you think everyone is meant to be with someone?"

"No. But only because some people seem happier when they're single."

"I can't imagine being married. Just thinking about it makes me panic."

Absolute proof that they were wrong for each other. "It has the opposite effect on me. The thought of being married makes me feel calm."

"Do you have the ceremony planned out in your

mind? The style of dress you'll wear and whatever else women daydream about?"

"Actually, I don't. I purposely haven't done that. Otherwise the wedding becomes more important than the marriage."

"That's a grounded way of thinking."

She appreciated his praise and even preened a little. "Thank you."

"Look at you. All pretty and smug. I still think your list is goofy."

"You're just miffed because I won't let you see it."

"Has anyone seen it?"

"I showed it to Tammy after she and Doc got together." She'd needed to confide in someone, and Tammy had been the logical choice. Sharing it with Donna would have been way too awkward.

"Can you blame me for wanting to see it? How am I supposed to leave the Flying B without knowing what type of man Jenna Byrd wants to marry?"

"You can come back someday and meet my husband."

"And tell him that we danced to 'Let's Make Love'?" You should pick that for your wedding song."

"Ha, ha. Very funny. And for the record, we haven't danced to it yet."

"We will. But if I'm a lousy dancer, it's going to ruin the song for you."

Maybe having it ruined would be better than feeling its sensual effect, she thought.

Just then, "Save a Horse (Ride a Cowboy)" came on, adding a bit of fuel to the fire. What timing. The crowd exploded with hoots and hollers and country wildness.

J.D. gestured to the table. "Hey. Manny and Maria are getting up."

She followed his line of sight. Sure enough, the younger couple was headed toward the dance floor.

"They must have picked this song," J.D. said.

"So it seems."

"Can't say as I blame them. They'll probably have a great time with it."

Jenna nodded. No doubt they would.

He kept watching. "Yep. There they go."

She watched, too. They were definitely having a great time. Whenever Maria would bump her hips, Manny would flash a big happy grin and mimic her movements. Jenna couldn't fathom scooting around to the song, while she was in the presence of the cowboy she'd vowed *not* to ride.

"Should we go back to the table?" he asked.

She nodded, and they resumed their seats. Then J.D. leaned over and quietly asked, "Do you think it's becoming obvious that we're attracted to each other?"

"Obvious to whom?"

"Whoever is around us."

She glanced at the Flying B employees who were left at the table. "I'm sure it will be when we dance. We're going to smolder, remember?"

"If I don't blow it."

"You won't."

"They'll probably talk about us."

"It doesn't matter." Instead of fretting about the curiosity that would ensue, she justified being gossiped about. "It's just an innocent flirtation. It's not as if we're going to go home together tonight."

He turned quiet, and the anxiety of waiting for the song they'd picked was almost too much to bear.

Then, about fifteen minutes later, it happened. The first melodic chords of "Let's Make Love" began to play.

Their gazes locked. Hard and deep.

It was time for them to dance.

Chapter Six

J.D. reached for Jenna's hand. "Ready?" he asked, even if he wasn't sure if he was ready himself.

"Yes." She accepted his hand and they walked onto the dance floor.

He took her in his arms and drew a blank. Here he was, holding a beautiful woman, and he still didn't know if he could dance. He couldn't seem to move, so he simply stood there, locked in position.

"Are you all right?" she asked.

"I'm more nervous than I thought I'd be."

"Do you want to forget it? You're under no obligation to—"

"No. I want to try." He listened to the melody, the lyrics, the singer's voice, letting those elements guide him. Slowly, he began to relax and dance with her.

A gentle, heart-stirring two-step.

Mercy, they were good together. Beyond good. Beyond imagination. They gazed at each other the entire time.

"You absolutely know how to do this," she said.

So did she, but her skills were never in question.

As they rocked and swayed, the other dancers barely existed and neither did the bar. Everything was out of focus, melding into misty colors and scattered light. All he saw was Jenna, her fair skin and golden hair.

He brought her closer. "I'm glad I met you. I'm even glad I lost my memory."

"I'm glad we met, too. But you shouldn't say that about having amnesia."

"It's giving me a chance to start over."

"This isn't starting over, J.D. It's a break from your other life."

"I don't care about my other life."

"You shouldn't say that, either. It's important to care about who you are."

How could he care about something he couldn't remember?

They didn't talk anymore, and he was grateful for the silence. He didn't want to disturb the bond. He wanted the luxury of knowing her in this way.

He was in the moment. He was part of it. *John Doe and Jenna Byrd,* he thought. He danced with her as if his amnesia depended on it, the heat between them surging through his veins.

This was a memory he would never forget.

When the song ended, his vision cleared and the bar came back into focus. But it didn't put him on solid ground. He longed to kiss Jenna, to taste her ruby-red lips.

"I need some air," he said. "How about you?"

"Definitely." She looked as dazed as he felt.

He escorted her outside, and they stood in front of the club, with a view of the parking lot. Other people were out there, too, standing off to the side and smoking, the tips of their cigarettes creating sparks.

Speaking of sparks...

J.D. was still feeling the fire. Apparently so was Jenna. Her voice vibrated. "I warned you that we were going to smolder. I've never danced with anyone like that before."

"I doubt I have, either." He struggled to put it in perspective. "How long do you think that song was?"

"Three, maybe four minutes."

"That's nothing in the scheme of things."

"I know. But it was beautiful." Her eyes drifted closed.

"Maybe you really should use it as your wedding song."

She opened her eyes. "I could never do that, especially not after dancing with you to it. That wouldn't be fair to my husband."

"Would it be fair to him if I became your short-term lover?" He couldn't help it. He wanted to have a dazzling affair with her. "I'd be good to you, the best lover I could be."

"I'm sure it would be amazing." She crossed her arms over her chest, and the protective gesture made her look achingly vulnerable. "But if we slept together, it would complicate my feelings for you, and I would miss you even more after you're gone."

Her reaction made him feel guilty for suggesting the affair. But he still wanted to be with her. Regardless, he said, "You're right. It wouldn't work. It wouldn't solve anything. We need to focus on being friends, like we agreed on from the beginning."

She nodded, but she didn't uncross her arms. She still looked far too vulnerable. He wanted to reach out and hold her, but he refrained from making physical contact. He'd done enough damage for one night.

He glanced at the smokers. They kept puffing away. As he shifted his attention back to Jenna, the headlights from a departing car shined in his eyes. He blinked from the invasion.

"I've never actually had an affair," she said.

He blinked again. He hadn't expected her to offer that kind of information.

She continued, "I've only been with two men and they were my boyfriends. Neither of them was right for me, though."

"They weren't husband material?"

"I thought they were at the time, but I misjudged them. That's part of why I created the list. I needed something definitive to use as a guide. I've always had specific ideas about family, considering how messed up mine was, and writing everything down was the best way I knew to stay focused on my priorities."

He considered the time line. She'd told him that she'd started the list when she was twenty-five and she was thirty now. "You haven't dated since then?"

"Yes, but just casually."

"So, you've been celibate for five years?"

"I'd rather wait for the right man. Besides, I haven't been overly attracted to anyone, not until…"

Dare he say it? "I came along?"

"Yes."

He blew out a gust of air from his lungs. She did, too, only in a softer manner. Still, they were mirroring each other.

Then, awkward silence.

The smokers stamped out their cigarettes and returned to the club, making it quieter.

More awkward silence.

"Maybe we should go back inside, too," he said.

A strand of hair blew across her cheek, and she batted it away. "I think I should go home, J.D."

And get away from him and their madly wrong-for-each-other attraction, he thought. "I'll walk you to your truck."

"Thanks." She led the way.

They didn't speak. The only sound was their booted footsteps.

Once her pickup came into view, she stated the obvious. "We're here." She hit the alarm button on her key fob.

If they were dating, this would have been the time to kiss her.

He made a point of keeping his distance. "Be safe."

"I will." She got in her truck and started the engine.

As she drove away, he gazed into the dark, feeling much too alone.

Jenna paced her room and finally ended up in the kitchen, heating milk in a pan on the stove. When she was little, her mother used to give her warm milk and now she thought of it as comfort food.

She poured it into a coffee mug and wandered the halls in her pajamas. It was after midnight, and she didn't expect to run into anyone else at this hour.

She was wrong. She noticed that one of the empty guest-room doors was open and a light was on. Jenna poked her head in and saw her sister.

She crossed the threshold and said, "What are you doing?"

Donna spun around, her hand flapping against her heart. "You scared the daylights out of me."

"Sorry, but it's not daylight." A dumb thing to say, she supposed, since that was a technicality of which they were both aware.

A beat of silence passed before Donna replied to her original question. "I have too much work on my mind to sleep."

"Is this the room that's going to overlook the garden?"

"Yes, and in my sleep-deprived state, I'm still debating on what wallpaper to use."

Jenna replied, "I couldn't sleep, either. Or relax or sit still. But I guess you already figured that out."

"What are you drinking? I hope it's not coffee. You'll be wired all night if it is."

"It's warm milk."

Donna didn't react. But to do so would have opened the door to a discussion about Mom, and Donna was apparently more cautious than that.

"I went out earlier," Jenna said.

"Where to?"

"Lone Star Lucy's."

Donna crinkled her nose. "That yee-haw bar? Whatever for?"

"Some of the ranch hands and maids were meeting there, and J.D. invited me, too. He invited all of us, you, me, Tammy and Doc, but I was the only one who could go."

"No one told me that I was invited."

"Would you have gone?"

"Not a chance."

"Then what would have been the point in telling you?"

"Protocol. I would have declined the invitation myself." Donna took a chair near the window. "Did that place live up to its reputation?"

Jenna sat on the edge of the bed. "Nothing crazy happened while I was there." Nothing except the way J.D. made her feel. "I left early, though."

"You weren't having a good time, I take it."

"Actually, I was enjoying myself." *Far too much,* she thought.

"Why is that a reason to leave early?"

"Because I danced with J.D. and then he suggested that we have an affair."

"You said that you didn't have a crush on him. I should have known you were lying."

Donna's reaction actually made her seem like a big sister. Or heaven forbid, a mother.

Jenna replied, "I'm not going to sleep with him."

"Right."

"I turned him down. I swear I did." She'd never confided in Donna about things like this before. Girl talk between them was a foreign concept. But she continued, hoping it was going to get easier. "I told him that it wasn't a good idea, and he agreed that we shouldn't."

"I'll bet he only agreed because you turned him down. If you would have said yes, you'd be doing it right now instead of roaming around in your pajamas.

Be honest, Jenna, you're having trouble sleeping because you want to climb into bed with him."

"Of course I want to. But I'm smart enough to know when to keep my pajamas on."

"They're pretty, by the way. A bit of silk, a bit of lace."

Jenna clutched her cup. She suspected that Donna had more to say about her sleepwear.

She did indeed. The older sibling added, "They're actually pretty enough to wear on a stroll down to his cabin and crack open those condoms I inadvertently provided."

"You're supposed to be talking me out of being with him, not tempting me to do it."

"I already tried to talk you out of it. I warned you that having a Flying B romance would be trouble, but you didn't listen. You danced with him anyway, a dance that prompted him to suggest an affair."

"He took it back."

"Uh-huh. Well, go traipse down to his cabin and see how quickly he jumps your bones."

Jenna scowled. Girl talk with her know-it-all New York sister sucked. "I'm going back to bed."

"Alone?"

"Yes, alone." Jenna stood up, preparing to stomp off.

Donna rolled her eyes. "You're acting like you did when we were kids."

"I am not."

"Yes, you are. You were always melodramatic."

"You mean like this?" For the heck of it, Jenna stuck out her tongue.

Donna shook her head, and they both laughed. Jenna

got a surge of warm and fuzzy, of the closeness that had been missing between them all these years.

But before she could bask in it, the moment ended and Donna withdrew again. She said a quiet good-night, and when she turned away, she stared out the darkened window. Was work the real reason she couldn't sleep? Or did she have something else on her mind?

Jenna went back to her room. Figuring out Donna was impossible when she could barely figure out herself.

She walked over to the mirror and gazed at her reflection. No way was she going to go to J.D.'s cabin dressed like this. Besides, he was probably still at the bar. Not that his whereabouts mattered.

She ditched her milk and got into bed, pulling the covers up around her ears. She was staying away from him for the rest of the night.

The following morning, Jenna finished up some work in the barn, but she didn't come across J.D. She didn't see him anywhere. Curious, she checked the schedule and discovered that it was his day off. She glanced at her watch. She planned on taking Pedro out for a trail ride, and if she brought J.D. along, he could ride Duke. Both horses needed to get away from the barn, and it would be good to take them out together.

Was that an excuse to see J.D., to spend time with him?

Maybe, but it was also important for her lesson horses to get accustomed to the trails. So why not kill two birds with one stone? It would be nice to pack a picnic, too, and enjoy a long leisurely ride.

She suspected that J.D. was anxious to put time in

the saddle, and this would be a great opportunity for him to do that, if he didn't have other plans for the day. The only way to know would be to ask him.

As she walked to his cabin, her heart started to pound, mimicking the erratic motion it had made when she'd danced with him. If only she could keep her attraction to him in check. But at least she'd had the good sense to refuse his offer of having an affair.

She arrived at his place, but instead of approaching the cabin, she sat on the bottom step, hoping to quiet her mind. But it didn't work. In that lone moment, she thought about Savannah Jeffries and her connection to the cabin. How could Savannah have had affairs with two men, brothers no less, when Jenna could barely contain her feelings for one man?

"Jenna?"

She stood up and spun around. J.D. stood in the doorway, gazing at her.

"Hi," she said, feeling foolish for getting caught off guard.

"What are you doing?" he asked.

Aside from wondering about Savannah? "I was just sitting here for a minute, before I came to see you. What are you doing?"

"I was planning on going for a walk."

She didn't ascend the steps. She stayed where she was. "Would you like to go for a ride instead? On horseback," she clarified so he didn't think she was inviting him to go somewhere in her truck. "I can ride Pedro, and you can ride Duke. We can take them out by the creek."

"Are you kidding? I'd love to. When?"

"We could go now, but I was thinking that we could

have lunch on the trail. I can head over to the main house and throw something together before we leave."

"Mind if I tag along?"

"Not at all. It would be nice to have the company."

He closed the cabin door and joined her.

While they walked beside each other, she asked, "How long did you stay at the bar last night?"

"Until it closed. I would have left earlier, but that's how long everyone else stayed and I didn't have a ride back."

She forged ahead into her next question. "Did anyone say anything?"

"About us? Everyone at the table did, especially Manny. He asked me if we were going to hook up, but I told him nó, that it was just a dance. It was an easy explanation."

"Do you think he bought it?"

"Why wouldn't he? It was the truth."

It wouldn't have been the truth if she'd agreed to sleep with him, but she kept that to herself. "I'm glad it's over."

"The explanation or the dance?"

Her heart thumped. "The explanation. The dance, too, but not because I didn't like it."

"I know you liked it, Jenna. We both did. But we probably shouldn't talk about it anymore."

Or think about it, she reminded herself.

Once they were in the kitchen, she opened the fridge. "Is ham and cheese okay, with lettuce, tomatoes and peperoncinis? That's about as fancy as I get."

"Sounds good to me. But my culinary skills aren't any better than yours." He watched her set everything on the counter. "Are you going to ask Tammy to teach you to cook?"

"Actually, I think I am. I'd feel better about being a wife and mother if I could offer my family some home-cooked meals now and then. Plus there's that old saying, 'The way to a man's heart is through his stomach.'"

"I'm still willing to be your guinea pig. I can give you an honest opinion and tell you if your lessons are working." He flashed his lopsided grin. "And if they aren't, Doc can pump my stomach."

"All in the name of helping me nab a husband? Oh, gee. That's mighty gentlemanly of you."

"It's the least I can do since I messed up your wedding song."

"That was never intended to be my wedding song." She jabbed his shoulder in a playful reprimand. "And we're not supposed to be talking about the dance, remember?"

His grin resurfaced. "Sorry. My bad."

"Very bad." But she understood his need to flirt. She was doing it, too, even if she knew better.

He offered to help, and they built the sandwiches together, working well as a team, unskilled as they were.

She snagged a pepper and ate it. "I love these."

He snagged one, too. "Spicy and sweet, like a girl I know."

More flirting. "You wish you knew her."

"A guy can dream."

"In the dream cabin? Those aren't the kinds of dreams that are supposed to happen there."

"Then I'm safe because I haven't done that yet."

Yet? She decided it was time to change the subject.

"We should get going or we're going to be starving by the time we make it to the creek."

He tossed a couple of apples into their lunch sacks. "I'm ready."

So was she. They went to the barn, saddled the horses and packed their saddlebags with food and water.

They rode for hours. The weather was perfect and the ever-changing terrain was riddled with towering trees, fallen branches, stony surfaces, grass, weeds and wildflowers.

J.D. was a magnificent horseman. He looked strong and regal on his mount. Jenna had to keep stopping herself from admiring him too deeply.

Upon reaching the creek, they set up their picnic, using a blanket they'd brought.

"This is beautiful," he said as a butterfly winged by.

"It's my favorite spot on the trail." She sat across from him. "Heaven on earth, as they say."

He unwrapped his sandwich. "I appreciate you sharing your favorite spot with me."

"That's what friends are for." She just wished that the platonic stuff was easier. "It's nice having a male friend to talk to."

"About finding a husband?"

"And other things." She removed the wrapping from her sandwich, too. "I was thinking about Savannah Jeffries earlier. That's what I was doing when you came out of the cabin and saw me. I think about her a lot."

"You actually haven't told me much about her, other than she was your uncle's girlfriend and Tammy discovered that she was keeping a secret."

"I can tell you the whole story now." Suddenly this seemed like the right time, the right place. "It's sordid, though." She steadied her emotions and started at the beginning. "Tammy first learned of Savannah when she overheard some of the household staff talking about her. Employees who've been around the Flying B a long time. Not like the young maids we socialized with at Lucy's."

He nodded in understanding.

She continued, "According to what Tammy overheard, Savannah didn't just sleep with Tammy's dad. She slept with mine, too."

"Damn," J.D. said.

Jenna's thoughts exactly. "Savannah was Uncle William's girlfriend when he was at Texas A&M, and that's why she was staying at the ranch. He was on summer break from university. He'd been in a car accident, and she came here to help him mend. My dad was home that summer, too."

"Giving Savannah the opportunity to mess around with him, too? That's some heavy stuff."

"It gets worse."

"I'm listening."

"Tammy uncovered an old grocery list in the cabin. It was from the time when Savannah was staying there."

"Why is that relevant?"

"It had an E.P.T. pregnancy test on it."

J.D. started. "That was her secret when she left town? She was pregnant?"

Jenna put her sandwich aside. "She might have been. But there's no way to know for sure. That's why we need to decide if we should hire a P.I. to search for her."

"The family vote?"

She nodded. "If Savannah was pregnant and she gave birth, then the child could belong to either man. Of course he or she wouldn't be a child anymore. They would be the oldest of all of us."

"I think you should hire the P.I."

"Really? Because I was going to vote no. As much as I want to uncover the truth, I'm afraid it will open a can of worms we're not prepared to deal with."

"I understand your concern, but I think it's important to know if there is another member of your family out there. Just think, Jenna, you could have another brother or sister. Or another cousin. That's epic."

Too epic, she thought.

He asked, "Are your dad and uncle going to vote on it, too?"

"No. Just the kids. Donna and I don't want our dad having a stake in it, so that means leaving Uncle William out of it, too. But he made his position clear. He would just as soon never see Savannah again. He's not trying to influence our vote, though. He'll accept whatever all of us decide."

"Does your dad want to see Savannah again?"

"I have no idea, and I don't intend to ask him. Donna and I are no longer on speaking terms with him."

He frowned. "So what's the holdup? Why haven't you voted yet?"

"We're waiting for Tammy's brothers to come back to the ranch. They went home after Tex's funeral and are scheduled to return next week. They have their own business. They're general contractors, and they've been busy with work. When they have time, they're going to help do some renovations around here."

"For the B and B?"

"Yes." She glanced at the body of water and the

way it shimmered. "Are you absolutely convinced that I should vote yes?"

"I would if I were you."

"Because family is important? You keep saying that yours doesn't matter because you can't remember them."

"That's because I don't think I have anyone."

She felt lonely for him, but confused for herself, too. Was he right? Should she vote yes?

"Tex hired a P.I. to keep an eye on all of us," she said. "He felt badly about not knowing his grandchildren, so he used someone to find out about us and report back to him."

"That's nice that he cared so much about you. I wonder if he would've condoned the use of a P.I. to find Savannah now that there's a possible child involved."

"I don't know." She pushed the P.I. out of her mind and moved on to a new topic. "Do you want to take a road trip with me this weekend? There's an equestrian center north of Houston that has some school horses for sale."

"Sure, that sounds great. Is it affiliated with the center where you used to work?"

"No. But it's a nice place, and they have some horses that are worth seeing. There's only one motel near there, so I'll book us a couple of rooms ahead of time."

"I can sleep in the truck."

Spoken like a true cowboy. "Humor me, J.D., and accept a room." She smiled. "Way far away from where mine will be."

He laughed. "On the other side of the motel, huh? It's a deal, if you let me buy you dinner while we're there."

"As long as there's no dancing involved."

"There won't be, I promise."

"Then it's a deal for me, too." She was determined to keep their upcoming trip friendly and light.

With absolutely no distractions.

Chapter Seven

The trip was long, but interesting. J.D. enjoyed Jenna's company. She was a hell of a woman: smart, pretty, funny, sweet. She knew how to handle a rig, too. She was driving a Dodge dually and gooseneck horse trailer that had belonged to her grandfather, with the Flying B brand prominently displayed.

They arrived in the evening, too late to go to the equestrian center. But they knew ahead of time that they would be cutting it close, so they'd already made arrangements to see the horses in the morning.

"Let's check into the motel, then get some dinner," she said. "In fact, there's a diner there where we can eat. Then we don't have to go back out again."

"Sure. That will work." He didn't blame her for wanting to stay put for the night. She'd been behind the wheel for hours.

The motel was a typical roadway-style place, located in a rural area. The restaurant next to it was a rustic building with a yellow rose painted in the window, and across the street was a gas station with a little convenience store.

She parked the truck and trailer. "The equestrian center is just up the road. It'll be easy to head over there in the morning."

"I'm sorry I wasn't able to help with the driving. You must be beat."

"I'm a little tired, but it's nothing a hot meal can't cure." She glanced over at him. "Besides, you'll be able to drive once your identity is restored and you have access to your driver's license. I wonder how long it will be before the police uncover anything."

"I don't know, but Deputy Tobbs is probably right about me having been carjacked and robbed. That scenario seems to make the most sense."

"Do you remember how to drive?"

"I have a sense of it. I'm sure that when I get behind the wheel it will feel natural."

They exited the truck and went into the rental office. The middle-aged woman behind the counter greeted them, and J.D. realized that they probably looked like a couple, as if they would be staying together. That was quickly dispelled. Jenna asked for two rooms.

Afterward, she handed him his key card. "Your room is next to mine."

For lack of a better response, he made a joke. "What happened to putting me in a room far, far away from yours?"

She smiled. "What can I say? It would have been weird. The clerk would have thought you were a leper."

"I'm just an amnesiac. That's not nearly as bad." He smiled, too. "You can't catch my forgotten memory."

Her expression turned somber. "Sometimes I wish I could."

He assumed that she was referring to the Savannah Jeffries scandal. "I'm sorry you're at odds with what's going on with your family."

"It helped talking to you about it."

"I'm glad you trusted me with your feelings."

"You're turning into a really good friend, J.D."

"So are you, Jenna."

A beat of intimacy passed between them, but she filled it quickly. "Are you ready to eat? We can bring our luggage into our rooms after dinner."

He nodded. His luggage was a duffel bag he'd borrowed from Manny, and hers was an airline-style carry-on with a push-button handle and wheels.

They entered the diner. It had the same rustic appeal inside as it did on the outside, with battered wood booths and antler light fixtures.

A hostess took them to a small corner booth, and they scooted in beside each other. J.D. studied the menu, but Jenna only glanced at hers.

"I already know what I want," she said. "I've got a hankering for a burger and fries. A chocolate milk shake, too."

"That sounds good. I'll get the same thing." He set his menu down. "But with a root-beer float."

The waitress arrived, and they placed their orders.

While they waited for the meals, he asked, "Where in Houston did you grow up?"

"It's about sixty miles from here. Mom stayed in our

old house after the divorce, and Dad got himself a new place, but it was in the same neighborhood."

"A suburban area?"

She nodded. "Near shopping malls and schools and everything else a family might want, I guess. I prefer the country. Always have, always will."

He glanced out the window. "I like this area. It has a great view."

"That's the Sam Houston National Forest in the distance."

"It's impressive."

"Yes, it is." She frowned. "My dad was named after Sam Houston. Sam Houston Byrd. My uncle's full name is William Travis Byrd. But less people know who William Travis is than Sam Houston. Dad got the biggie."

She always scowled when she mentioned her father, but he understood why, considering the Savannah situation. Still, he wished it wasn't troubling her so badly. "You should discuss the details with your dad."

"The details?"

"About what happened all those years ago."

"I don't want to hear about his dirty little fling with his brother's girlfriend."

"I'm talking about the impact it had on his life and the family rift it caused, not the physical stuff between him and Savannah."

She set her jaw. "I know what you meant."

Dang, she was stubborn. "I'm just saying that maybe you should try to make things right with your dad."

"I'm not going to right his wrong."

"There are two sides to every story."

"His side isn't a story I care to hear."

He decided to drop it for now, with the intention of

broaching the subject another time. The way this was gnawing at her wasn't healthy.

During the lapse in conversation, their food and drinks arrived. She dived in, as eager as a bear coming out of hibernation.

"I'm sorry for getting testy," she said.

"You'll feel better now that you're getting some chow in you."

"It's yummy. The milk shake, especially." She sipped from a red-and-white-striped straw.

"My root-beer float is good, too."

She smiled. "Sugar highs."

He could get high on her smile, if he let himself. Let himself? Hell, he already was.

As a distraction, J.D. looked out the window again, where the view erupted into hills, valleys and scores of trees.

She followed his line of sight. "I hope you didn't get the impression that I'm at odds with the real Sam Houston. It's not his fault that my dad ended up with his name."

"I didn't think you disliked *Colonneh*."

"What? Who?"

He blinked, as confused as she was. He didn't know why he'd said *Colonneh.* Not until his thoughts jumbled into a feeling, a memory, and struck him like a warrior's arrow. "Oh, God, Jenna, I'm related to him."

"I don't know who you're talking about."

He turned to look at her. "Sam Houston."

He gaped at him. "*The* Sam Houston?"

"Well, not him, exactly. But to the band of Cherokee that adopted him."

Another gape. "You're Cherokee?"

"Part. A quarter," he added, amazed by how quickly this information was tumbling into his mind. "That's how I'm registered with the tribe."

"And you're certain that you're affiliated with the band that adopted Sam?"

"Yes. This stuff just hit me, memories that zoomed into my head." And it made him damned proud, too. "Pretty cool, huh?"

"I'll say." She studied him with awe. "Was *Colonneh* Sam's Cherokee name?"

He nodded. "It means The Raven."

"Oh, that's right. His other name was Raven. All Texans should know that. But to actually know someone whose ancestry is connected to his…" She paused. "Do you recall anything else about yourself? Like who told you about your heritage?"

"No. But I'm from Texas. I'm not sure what part I hail from, but it's my homeland." He smiled, feeling a bond with the Lone Star State, with Sam, with the Cherokee blood running through his veins.

"I'm happy for you, J.D."

As she leaned toward him, his heart knocked against his chest. She was almost close enough to kiss. All he had to do was make his move to close the deal. He studied her mouth, then lifted his gaze. She was staring at him, too.

"We aren't supposed to be doing this," she said.

"We aren't doing anything but looking at each other."

"But we want to do more."

"We've wanted that since the beginning."

"We can't."

"We could," he corrected. "But we agreed that we wouldn't."

Regardless, they were damn close to breaking their agreement. She even wet her lips. Unable to help himself, so did he. But then Jenna moved away from him and grabbed her milk shake, sucking viciously on the straw. Unfortunately, her diversion didn't help. It only managed to give him a wildly sexual feeling, worsening his urges.

After their meal ended, they got their luggage from the truck and proceeded to their rooms. But they didn't unlock their doors. They just stood there, trapped in their attraction.

"We better go," she said.

He motioned with his chin. "You first."

She fumbled for her key card, digging around in her purse. She found it and gripped the plastic a little too tightly. "I'll see you in the morning."

"Okay." He didn't trust himself to say anything else. He was still thinking about her mouth on the straw or, more accurately, about kissing her senseless.

She went inside, and he waited until she closed the door before he blew out his breath.

And wished that he was spending the night with her.

Jenna stood in the middle of her room, wondering how long it would take J.D. to enter his. *This is crazy,* she thought, *absolute insanity.* She wanted to forgo their friendship pact and become lovers.

Then why not do it? Honestly, what did she have to lose?

Her heart, for one thing. If she fell in love with him, she would be setting herself up for a world of pain. It wasn't as if J.D. was going to stick around and marry her.

But he wasn't even husband material, so what was the likelihood of falling in love with him, anyway? There was nothing wrong with uncommitted sex. True, it wasn't Jenna's style, but maybe she needed to re-think her immediate priorities. Later, she could find a man who had the qualities on her list. Later, she could walk down the aisle with Mr. Right. But at the moment, *Mr. Right Now* was *right* next door.

Still, she stalled.

Needing more time to contemplate the issue, she stripped off her clothes and drew a hot bath. Determined to relax, she pinned up her hair and soaked in the tub. She even closed her eyes. Then she lost all sense of rea-son and conjured an image of J.D. pulling her into his arms. So much for contemplating the issue. She knew darned well that she was going to cave into temptation.

Should she invite him to her room or go to his? Jenna didn't have any experience at this sort of thing.

She sat upright and scrubbed clean, careful not to get amorous with the soap. Touching herself wouldn't help her cause.

After drying off, she moisturized her skin. She brushed her teeth, refreshed her face and let down her hair, too.

Maybe it would be better to invite him over. That way she didn't have to get dressed. She could wrap her-self in her robe and stay naked underneath.

What if he rebuffed her advances?

Oh, sure. As if that was going to happen. She knew that J.D. wanted this as badly as she did.

She slipped on her robe, a silky garment that ca-ressed her flesh. Better though, would be the sensa-tion of J.D.'s hands.

Without further hesitation, she dialed his room.

He answered on the second ring. "Hello?"

"It's me," she said, instead of reciting her name. Who else would be calling him at the motel? "I was wondering if you wanted to come over and hang out."

A slight pause. "For how long?"

Here goes, she thought. "All night. I want to be with you, J.D."

His voice turned graveled. "Are you sure?"

Her nerves jangled. "Yes."

"I just got out of the shower." His voice remained rough, anxious, sexy. "I need to get dressed."

Was he fully naked? Or did he have a towel tucked around his waist? She didn't have the courage to ask. Instead, she said, "I just got out of the bath. And I'm in my robe." Fair warning, she decided. No surprises.

"Damn. I'll hurry. But first I have to run across the street to the convenience store."

Obviously he intended to buy condoms. The motel didn't provide them, not like Donna had done for the guest accommodations at the ranch.

"I can't believe this is going to happen," he said. "Are you sure you're not going to change your mind?"

"I'm positive." She didn't have the strength to back out. She needed him, more than anything. "I'll see you soon."

They ended the call with eager goodbyes, and she returned to the bathroom to check her appearance. She even opened her robe and looked at her naked self in the mirror.

Her nerves went nuts. What if he found her lacking? What if he thought her hips were too bony or her breasts were too small? Dang it, why hadn't she been blessed with a figure like her sister's?

Jenna closed her robe and tied the belt. She couldn't do anything about her body. She was what she was.

She headed for the bed and sat on the edge of it. He'd said that he would hurry, but it felt like forever.

Finally, a knock sounded on the door.

She leaped up and answered it. There stood J.D. with a small paper bag in one hand and a plastic yellow rose in the other. Their gazes locked, and he extended the rose.

He said, "It's not the prettiest flower, but it's all they had."

She accepted his gift, assuming that the convenience store was selling them as souvenirs. "I think it's wonderful that you thought of me." And she would cherish the rose, simply because he gave it to her. "Come in, J.D."

He crossed the threshold and closed the door. Silence sizzled between them. He glanced down at her robe, particularly at the area where it gapped in front, revealing the hint of flesh between her breasts.

She didn't make an effort to close the material. Nor did she feel self-conscious about her lack of cleavage. He obviously liked what he saw.

He said, "Promise me that you won't have regrets later."

"I promise."

"What about the comment you made before?"

She considered his question. "You mean on the night we danced?"

He nodded, repeating her words and making them clear. "You said that if you slept with me, you would get attached and it would only make my leaving more difficult for you."

She replied as honestly as she could. "That crossed my mind tonight. I even considered how terrible it would be if I fell in love with you. But it's become more difficult wanting you than not having you, so I'm not going to worry about the future. All that matters is the here and now."

He reached out to touch her cheek. "Someday you'll find the man you're meant to marry."

"I'm counting on it."

But that didn't mean that she didn't appreciate him, exactly as he was, at this very moment. His hair was damp from the shower and although he'd combed it back, stray pieces fell on to his forehead. His hasty attire consisted of jeans, an untucked shirt, no belt and his usual battered boots.

He removed the condoms from the bag and opened the box. "I'm going to put these beside the bed for when we need them."

She handed him the flower. "Will you put the rose there, too?"

He set everything on the nightstand and returned to her. Then he took her into his arms and kissed her. The kiss she'd been waiting for. The kiss he'd been hungry to give her. Their lips met softly at first, but he deepened the contact quickly, using his tongue to intensify the feeling.

She flung her arms around his neck, and he held her body close to his. She could smell a citrus aroma—the customary soap from the motel—on his skin. She'd bathed with the same type of soap, and somehow that made their union seem even more sensual.

J.D. released the tie on her robe and the garment drifted open. He stepped back to look at her, and her heart thudded in her ears.

"Take it all the way off," he said.

Suddenly she went shy, her self-consciousness kicking in. But she did his bidding and removed the robe so he could fully see her.

"I should have put the lights on low," she said.

"No. It's perfect like this. You're perfect. Turn around."

She made what she hoped was a ladylike pirouette. When she faced him once again, he was smiling. She smiled, too. His crooked grin was infectious.

He anxiously led her to bed.

She watched while he discarded his clothes. They reclined on the mattress and started kissing again. Only now, caressing was involved. He roamed his hands along the lines of her body, making her skin tingle. She stroked him, too, gliding over flesh and bone and strong male muscle.

"I can't remember being with anyone else," he said. "But I'm glad I can't. I want this to be my first intimate memory."

His words affected her as deeply as his touch. "You certainly haven't forgotten how to entice a woman."

"You make me want to entice you."

He climbed on top, pinning her hands above her head and making her his willing prisoner. She studied his features. Now that she knew about his Cherokee roots, his heritage seemed magnificently obvious.

"Being with you is everything I imagined," she said.

"For me, too." He released her, but only because he

was moving down her body and making a moist path with his tongue.

She arched and closed her eyes. He did things a man had no right to do, things that ignited a fire, things that made her melt all over him. By the time she opened her eyes, she could barely see straight.

He reached for the protection, ripped into a packet and sheathed himself. He was impatient, but so was she. She didn't want to wait another second.

He entered her, and their lovemaking took flight, with Jenna matching his glorious rhythm. As she moved her hips in time with his, prisms of colors spun in her mind, binding them together, almost as if they were one.

But they weren't, she told herself. This was a pleasure-only affair. No heartstrings, no commitment, no ties. J.D. wasn't hers to keep.

And he never would be.

Chapter Eight

J.D. couldn't keep his eyes off Jenna. He wanted to devour her in every way imaginable. The experience was so new, so exciting.

He said, "Have you ever heard someone say that sex is overrated? Well, that's not true. Not when it makes you feel this way."

In lieu of a response, she wrapped her legs around him, and the experience got better and better.

He glanced down at her, intrigued by the sinuous manner in which she moved. Her skin was creamy and smooth, soft and fair and so unlike his. The wonderment was almost too much to bear, but she seemed as fascinated by him as he was by her.

She said, "I'm so glad you remembered something about yourself tonight."

"At least I know that I'm from Texas."

"Not only are you from here, you have a connection to Sam Houston. That makes the yellow rose you gave me even more special."

"Next time it will be a real flower. I'd give you hundreds of roses if I could."

"I always imagined rose petals on my honeymoon. All over the bed."

"Don't put fantasies like that in my head."

"You're not interested in marriage, J.D."

"No, but I like the flower-petals idea. It sounds sexy."

"And romantic."

"That, too." He covered her mouth with his. He also slipped his hand between them and heightened her pleasure.

Heat. Beautiful urgency.

He ached to give her a release, to shower her with everything she needed, everything she desired. They weren't a couple, nor were they on their way to becoming one, but for now they belonged to each other, and that was an aphrodisiac neither of them could deny.

Enthralled, he watched her, and with carnality bursting at the seams, she shuddered and climaxed. Unable to hold back, he lost himself in the passion, too.

Spent, he fell into her arms and stayed there for a while, allowing her to bask in the afterglow. She nuzzled his chest, her hair tickling his skin. In a deliberate show of affection, he skimmed a hand down her spine.

After they broke apart, he went into the bathroom to dispose of the condom.

He returned to find her sitting up in bed, with the quilt tucked around her. She looked sweetly tousled. Well-loved.

No! Not loved. He frowned at the mind slip. Making love wasn't love. In this case, it was miles apart.

Before she noticed his unease, he softened his expression and approached her. "Do you want a cup of tea? They have the herbal stuff."

"That sounds good."

He used the coffeepot to heat the water. He didn't brew himself any. He didn't drink hot tea. In fact, he wasn't sure why he'd offered some to her. Was it to keep his mind in check? Or was there someone from his past who favored tea? He honestly didn't know. In spite of his Sam Houston breakthrough, the bulk of his memories remained blocked.

"Cream and sugar?" he asked.

"Sugar. One packet."

He fixed the drink and brought it to her. "It's chamomile. It's supposed to be soothing."

She took the cup and tasted the fragrant brew. "It's just right. Thank you."

He sat beside her, his thoughts drifting back to the flower conversation, as well as to something she'd previously said. "You told me that you haven't planned any of your wedding details. But you have."

"The rose petals on the bed? I saw that in a movie, and it appealed to me. But we shouldn't do it. It wouldn't be right for our affair."

Because it would make their affair seem like a honeymoon? "I agree that we shouldn't."

She made a perplexed expression. "Funny, how we're always talking about what we shouldn't do."

"That's because we're being noncommittal."

She nodded, then clutched the tea with both hands,

as if she needed an extra dose of warmth. Was she thinking about the man she was destined to marry and wishing he was here instead? Or was J.D. the only man on her mind?

Either way, he said, "If you want to snuggle, I can hold you tonight while you sleep."

"That would be wonderful." She leaned against his shoulder. "I like to spoon."

"Me, too. I think." He tossed out a smile. "I can't remember. But I'm sure I'll like it with you."

Soon they settled in for sleep, extinguishing the lamp and taking the aforementioned spooning position, with the front of his body pressed against the back of hers. He slipped an arm around her waist, creating a cozier connection.

She sighed, the feathery sound proof of her contentment. Grateful that she was satisfied, J.D. whispered a gentle, "Good night."

"You, too," she responded, using an equally soft voice. She tugged at the covers, getting more comfortable.

Although he closed his eyes, he wasn't able to sleep, at least not right away. He could tell when Jenna drifted off, though, mostly by the change in her breathing. Her limbs seemed looser, too.

Finally he joined her, and in the morning, he awakened before she did. With dawn peeking through a space in the drapes, he sat up and gazed at his lover.

Such delicate repose, he thought, tempted to touch her. But he kept his hands at his sides. He didn't want to rouse her. He wanted to see her while she was unable to see him. He realized that it was his way of shielding his confused self from her, of continuing to hide behind his amnesia.

And taking an odd sort of comfort in it.

As Jenna awoke, she sensed that she was being watched. She squinted, struggling to get her bearings. Then she saw J.D. sitting next to her, the sheet draped around his waist, his dark gazed fixed on hers.

"Morning," he said, skimming his thumb along her cheek, as if he'd been waiting all morning to do that.

"Hi," she replied quickly, reminding herself not to get attached. Thing was, she wanted to grab him and never let go. But what woman wouldn't feel that way, considering how affectionate he was?

He took his hand away. "You still look sleepy."

She sat up and clutched her portion of the sheet, shielding her nakedness, more out of caution than shyness. "I suppose I am. What time is it?" She couldn't see the clock from her side of the bed.

"A little after six."

"Dang. I hadn't planned on getting up this early. We're keeping rancher's hours, even on a road trip. But I guess it stands to reason, considering we live on a ranch."

"I don't live at the Flying B, Jenna."

"You live there for now." Everything was temporary: his job, his living arrangements, their affair.

"You're right. I do." He leaned closer. "Can I kiss you? Or is it too early for that?"

Her pulse spiked. "It's never too early for a kiss."

He reached for her, and she released the sheet, allowing it to fall to her waist. Their mouths met and mated, and she slipped deeper into the moment.

There was no denying it; she was getting attached. But she would do her darnedest to cope with his departure when the time came.

Sweet and tender, the kiss continued. J.D. had a way of making her feel special, even if it wasn't meant to last.

He pushed the sheet completely away, making it easier to roll over the bed and take her with him. She landed on top, and he smiled. He obviously wanted to make love in this position.

But so did Jenna. She desired him in all sorts of ways. Her heart pounded from the want, the need, the anticipation.

He secured a condom, and the shiny packet glittered. He opened it and concentrated on his task. She suspected that they were going to go through the protection quickly.

"I'm glad we have more of those back at the ranch," she said.

He glanced up and smiled again, a bit more devilish this time. "That's for sure. Now let's get you seated, nice and tight."

He circled her waist, giving her a boost while she straddled him. She impaled herself, and the sensation nearly knocked her for a loop.

With a powerful grip, he lifted her up and down, setting a rocking horse rhythm. "You look like a cowgirl."

She latched on to his shoulders, mesmerized by his broad strength. "I feel like one, too."

"We're good together." He kept her within his grasp. "And it's good that there aren't any future worries between us."

"You mean no plans to stay in touch after you leave?" *No phone calls, emails, texts,* she thought.

He nodded, morning shadows playing against his skin. "You're still okay with that, right?"

"Yes." She was determined to accept it, the best she could. After he was gone, she would accept the blessing of having known him and move on with her life. "All I want right now is to make this happen."

He kissed her hard and rough. "Then do it. Make it happen."

Quickening the pace, she rode him with every ounce of hunger she had, bucking wildly, and leaving them both breathless when it was over.

J.D. took a minute to collect his thoughts, then he said to Jenna, "You blow me away."

"Likewise. Sex with you packs a punch." She climbed off his lap and sagged like a rag doll.

"Relax and I'll be right back." He got rid of the condom and returned to her. "Do you want me go to the diner and get some breakfast?"

"Sure. I'll shower while you're gone."

"I need to shower, too, and shave. But I left my bag in the other room."

"You can do that before you get breakfast. It will probably take me longer to get ready than you, anyway."

"Women and their hair and makeup." He twined his fingers around her golden locks. "I like you the way you are."

"Messy from going cowgirl?"

"Definitely." He noticed that her mouth was swollen from his kisses. Talk about hot. And sinful. And beautiful.

After a beat of soul-stirring silence, she pushed at his chest. "You better go. Before we end up ravishing each other again."

"Good thinking. Or else we'll never leave this bed."

"They'd find us, dead from exhaustion."

He laughed. "With a plastic rose and a box of condoms beside us. How embarrassing would that be?"

She laughed, too. "Proof that we need to control ourselves."

"And eat and be normal?" He climbed into his rumbled clothes. "What should I bring back for you?"

"Ham and eggs, with any kind of toast. It doesn't matter."

"How do you like your eggs?"

"Scrambled is fine."

He gave her a quick kiss, but it didn't satisfy the urges stirring inside him. He wanted to linger, to get his second wind, even after the jokes they'd made.

He headed for the door instead. He was too damned eager to have her again. But what did he expect? He couldn't remember being with anyone but Jenna.

He glanced back and saw that she was watching him. She even chewed her swollen lips, pulling the bottom one between her teeth. Neither of them had the affair down pat. She seemed overwhelmed, too, and possibly on the verge of telling him to forget breakfast and come back to her.

But she didn't give in. And neither did J.D.

He went to his room, and after he showered, shaved and donned clean jeans and a fresh shirt, he walked to the diner and ordered their meals.

Food in hand, he returned to Jenna and noticed that the door was ajar. She'd obviously left it that way for him. He entered the room. She was fully dressed, crisp and pretty in a Western blouse and jeans, with her hair in a ponytail.

"That's a good look on you," he said.

"Thank you."

The certified riding instructor, he thought. She definitely fit the part. The whole purpose of this trip was to shop for lesson horses, not have lust-burning sex.

He put the food on the dining table, which was positioned by the window and equipped with two padded chairs. "Okay if I open the drapes and let more light in?"

"Oh, of course. I meant to do that." She glanced at the takeout containers. "Which one is mine?"

"They're both the same. Ham and eggs was the special, with home-fried potatoes. I got wheat toast and lots of jelly to go with it. Ketchup and salt and pepper, too."

"I made coffee while you were gone. Do you want a cup?"

"Sure." He could use some caffeine. "Did you drink yours already?"

"No. I was waiting for you to come back." She poured two cups and set them on the table, along with the little basket that contained powdered creamer, sugar and the accompanying stir sticks.

They sat across from each other and fixed their coffee. Next, they opened the plastic utensils he'd gotten from the diner and doctored their meals. He squeezed ketchup on his eggs, and she used it on her potatoes. Both were generous with the pepper and light on the salt. She favored the grape jelly, and he went to town on the strawberry.

Would this be considered post-sex compatibility? *No,* he thought. *Not quite.*

She took deliberately small bites. She wasn't as ravenous as she'd been at dinner last night. Either that or she was trying to behave properly. He was, too, still mindful of his hunger for her.

She lifted her coffee and studied him from beneath the rim of her cup. "I wonder if you know any other Cherokee words besides Sam Houston's Raven name."

"It's possible, I suppose. Who knows what's locked inside my brain? But I should probably count my blessings that I remember how to speak English, let alone my ancestor's language."

"My ancestors are from Sweden. On my mom's side. The Byrds are Texans, through and through, but they originated from England, with a little gypsy tossed in. I didn't know about the gypsy part until Tex told us about our great-grandmother and the feather bed."

"It was foolish of me not believe in your great-grandmother's magic when you first mentioned it to me. The Cherokee believe in magic, in dreams, in visions. It's part of my culture, too. A medicine man is a called *di da nv wi s gi,* and it means 'curer of them.'"

"So you *do* know more Cherokee words."

"Well, damn. Listen to me." He grinned, stunned and pleased that it came so easily. "I guess I do."

She reached across the table to touch his hand. "It's nice to see you looking so happy."

"It's nice for me, too." And so was her caring touch.

"You know what, J.D.? I don't think you were a foster child. I think someone in your family taught you about your culture, and I think you were surrounded by it."

"You could be right. If I was a foster kid, I would probably be missing the Cherokee side of myself instead of recalling it in such a positive way."

As their hands drifted apart, she said, "It's still odd, though, that you seem to have knowledge of the foster-care system and how the older kids rarely get adopted."

"Maybe I knew someone else who grew up in that world."

"Someone who must have been important to you."

The tea drinker, perhaps? If there was such a person. "I don't know. It's all a bit weird. If I had a family, parents who nurtured me, maybe even brothers and sisters, then why do I get the sense of not having anyone in my life?"

"Maybe you just haven't remembered them yet."

"Or maybe something went wrong with my relationship with them. Maybe they turned away from me or I turned away from them. The positive connection I feel to my heritage doesn't mean that other aspects of my life aren't screwed up. Maybe I'm holding on to my heritage so tightly because it's all I have."

"I agree that there's something going on with your family. Otherwise you probably wouldn't be advising me to vote in favor of finding Savannah and the child she might have had. And you wouldn't be trying to encourage me to give my father a chance."

"Are you having a change of heart? Are you going to take my advice?"

"I'm considering the vote."

"But not squaring things with your dad? Sleeping with his brother's girlfriend was a lousy thing to do. But judging him without hearing his side of the story isn't fair, either."

"There's nothing he could say that would make me feel okay about what he did."

"Then forgive him to lessen the burden on yourself."

"I wish I could, but I can't." She moved a forkful of eggs around, mixing them with her potatoes. "If only my mom was still alive. I would talk to her about this if I could." She paused, apparently considering how the conversation would go. "If she were here, I think she would tell me to stay away from Dad and just let him be."

"Why do you think she would say that?"

"Because she never pushed Donna to open up. She accepted that my sister was distant, like Dad in that regard."

Curious, he asked, "Does Donna favor him in her appearance, too? Because I envision that you look more like your mom. And since you and Donna don't really resemble each other, I figure each of you took after a different parent."

"You got that right. I'm my mother's daughter."

He hadn't meant to imply that she didn't have anything in common with her father. "What does your dad think about you and Donna turning the ranch into a B and B?"

"He hasn't given us his opinion. But we don't want him butting into our business or trying to talk to us."

"When's the last time you saw him?"

"At Tex's funeral."

"If I were him, I would be proud of you and your sister. You make a hell of a team. And Tammy. The three of you are going to make the B and B a tremendous success."

Her eyes lit up. "Thanks. That means a lot to me. And thanks for caring about my feelings. Even if I don't follow your advice, I appreciate your motives." She motioned between them. "You and I make a good team, too. I'm glad I brought you on this trip and that you're going to check out the horses with me."

"So am I." He was eager to go to the equestrian center and help her in any way he could, and he couldn't agree more—they were a damned fine team.

In and out of bed.

Chapter Nine

Jenna hit the jackpot. She'd purchased two wonderful geldings and now she and J.D. were almost home, traveling down the Flying B Road and heading toward the ranch.

She glanced at the man she'd spent the night with. They'd behaved in a professional manner at the equestrian center. No hand-holding, no public display of affection, nothing that indicated that they were lovers.

"What's going to happen now that we're back?" she asked. "How are we going to handle this?"

"What do you mean?"

"Our affair. Are we going to sneak around and keep it a secret? Or let everyone know that we're together?"

"I'll do whatever you're comfortable with."

"What would you prefer?" Before she went out on a

limb and expressed her feelings, she desperately wanted
to know how he felt.

"Truthfully? I'd like to be open about it. We're both
consenting adults and have a right to be together. We
don't have anything to hide, not as far as I'm concerned.
But if you would rather go the secret route, I'll respect
your wishes."

He'd said exactly what she'd hoped he would say. "I
completely agree. Sneaking around seems cheap, and
it would make me feel cheap. I don't want to call dirty
attention to ourselves, and if we have a secret affair and
get caught, it will seem too much like what my dad did
with Savannah. Even if the circumstances aren't the
same, it would affect me that way."

"I'd never want to do anything that would make you
feel badly about yourself." He leaned over and kissed
her cheek. "This is a nice thing we've got going."

She smiled. "Very nice."

They arrived at the ranch, and she drove to the barn.
Although it was still daylight, dusk would be closing
in soon. As they prepared to unload the first gelding,
Manny and Hugh, who'd been working nearby, mo-
seyed on over to greet them, obviously curious about
the horses she'd purchased.

Jenna got a little nervous. She knew that she
shouldn't, not after she and J.D. agreed that they had
every right to disclose their affair, but now that they
were actually in the company of Flying B employees,
she wasn't sure how to act.

J.D. behaved in a perfectly natural way. He unloaded
the horse and talked to Hugh and Manny about both
geldings and what great finds they were. By the time
the second horse was unloaded and placed in his stall,

Jenna was able to relax, too. She realized that J.D. was going to handle it.

He said to the other men, "Normally I wouldn't bring something like this up, but I'm concerned about ranch gossip. Jenna and I are dating now. So if you notice us hanging around together or Jenna coming and going from my cabin more often than she did before, please treat the situation with respect."

Hugh replied, "I understand. People talk, and you can't stop their tongues from wagging. But you don't want them talking out of turn." He addressed Jenna. "I'll admit that I've done my share of talking over the years. But never in a hurtful way. And I won't do that to you, either."

"Thank you." She couldn't be more pleased with his reaction. Hugh was as honest as they come, and he'd been around since the Savannah days, witnessing the devastation firsthand.

Young Manny was another story. The Savannah situation had occurred long before he'd been born. No doubt he'd heard about it, though, especially since the past had been unearthed. But Manny only seemed concerned with the here and now.

A cheeky grin broke out on his face, and he said to Jenna, "I knew you two were going to hook up. Maria and I are seeing each other now, too. We should go on a double date sometime."

"Sure." She smiled at him. "Maria seems like a nice girl."

"She's the best. I'm right crazy for her."

Jenna hoped J.D. was feeling the same sense of boyish craziness for her, regardless of how short-lived their affair proved to be. She glanced over at him, and he winked, making her heart spin.

Hugh nudged Manny. "Let's go. It's about quitting time."

Manny was still grinning. To the new lovers, he said, "See you guys."

After the old foreman and the young ranch hand were gone, Jenna spoke to J.D. "Thanks for taking care of that."

"You're welcome. I figured that we needed to get it out there, better sooner than later." He reached for her hand. "Do you want to stay with me tonight? Or are you planning on sleeping in your own bed?"

"I'd like to stay with you, as long as you don't think it's too soon."

"Too soon for what? We already went public with it. In fact, maybe you should just move in with me."

Stunned, she stared at him. "Move in?"

"To the cabin. It would be nice to have you there every night, and now that my memory is starting to improve…"

"You only remembered a few things. Granted, they were really important things, but it was just bits and pieces."

"Yes, but look how quickly it happened. It's probably just a matter of time before everything comes rushing back. And then I'll be leaving."

"So we should cram in as many days together as we can?"

"It works for me."

It worked for her, too. She wanted as much of him as she could get and for as long as she could get it. Still, it wasn't something she'd expected. "I'll move in with you, but I need time to prepare. I want to talk to Donna and Tammy first."

"About us?"

She nodded. "I can't go skipping off to stay with you without explaining it to them."

He laughed. "Skipping?"

She play-punched his arm. "You know what I mean."

"Yes, I believe I do." He kissed her, long and slow, and she wrapped her arms around him.

After the kiss ended, she said, "Will you take my luggage to the cabin? There's no point in me hauling it back to the house. I should probably pack a few more bags if I'm moving in with you." She paused to ponder the situation. "God, that sounds weird. Us living together."

"I know, but I figure it's going to be more like a vacation since it's probably going to be so short."

"That's a good way of looking at it."

"It will be fun. A romantic adventure."

"I think so, too." One more kiss, and they parted ways.

As she exited the barn, the horses she'd just purchased whinnied, calling out to each other and adjusting to their new home. Jenna was making an adjustment, too.

She walked to the house with an emotionally cluttered mind. She came to the porch and ascended the steps, grateful that she owned a piece of the ranch. If J.D. was the type who wanted to settle down, she could easily imagine sharing her home with him.

But he wasn't, and it was pointless to entertain those types of imaginings. Someday she would meet the man from her list. J.D. wasn't him, and all of the wishing in the world wouldn't change the nature of their relationship. She had no choice but to accept it.

She opened the front door and saw Donna, sitting on the sofa, tapping away on her iPad. Although she was dressed casually, she managed to look elegant, as always.

Tammy was in the living room, too, paging through a magazine. She looked lovely, as well, and appeared to be dressed to go out. On the floor beside her was her purse.

Jenna approached both women. She was glad that she'd come across them together, rather than having to summon a meeting or speak to them separately.

Tammy glanced up first. "Hey," she said. "You're home from your trip. How did it go?"

Obviously Jenna had plenty to say about the subject, but she started off simple. "I bought some new lesson horses."

"That's great. Maybe I can see them tomorrow? I don't have time tonight. I'm waiting for Mike to call—we're meeting in town for dinner."

"Tomorrow would be fine. I'd like for you to see them." She didn't make the same offer to Donna. Her sister's allergies acted up whenever she went near the stables.

But that didn't stop Donna from sensing there was more to the conversation than met the eye. She asked, "What else is going on? Besides the horsey stuff?"

"A lot." Jenna sat beside her, with Tammy directly across from them. "I took J.D. on the trip with me, and we're lovers now. But it's just an affair."

Tammy frowned. "There's no commitment involved?"

"He isn't the right man for that."

Donna put the iPad down. "I figured that you'd end up sleeping together. It was obvious how much you wanted him."

"As long as you don't get hurt," Tammy put in.

"I won't. After he leaves, I'll go on with my life and he'll go on with his." She dropped the rest of her bomb. "But we're going to live together for the duration of his stay. I'm moving into the dream cabin with him, and we're going to treat it as a vacation, of sorts."

"That sounds too easy," Donna said.

Before a feeling of sadness crept in, Jenna shoved it away. "Actually, J.D is getting closer to recouping his memory." She relayed the Sam Houston/Cherokee information. "He thinks it's only a matter of time before the rest of it comes tumbling back."

Tammy scooted to the edge of her chair. "That's fascinating. Okay if I tell Mike? He should know."

"I'm sure that would be fine. I think J.D. would appreciate you passing it on to Doc. Come to think of it, J.D. should probably inform Deputy Tobbs, too. The more information the sheriff's department has, the better their chances are of uncovering his identity. In case he doesn't remember everything on his own."

After a stream of silence, Tammy said, "This is off topic, but I already told Donna while you were on your trip, and it concerns the three of us. I heard from my brothers this morning. They'll be here on Wednesday, so if that fits into your schedule, we should plan on having the vote that day."

Jenna's stomach went tight. The P.I. Savannah. The possible child. "J.D. thinks I should vote yes. He thinks it's important to know the truth and embrace it."

Tammy replied, "That's what I'm going to do," making her upcoming vote apparent.

Donna scrunched up her face, indicating an opposing opinion.

Jenna said, "I haven't made a decision, but I'm leaning toward yes. I'm curious about Savannah, but I'm even more curious if there's another Byrd out there. What if it's someone who needs a family? Who would like to have us be part of his or her life?"

"What if it's someone who doesn't?" her sister countered. "If another other Byrd exists, he or she could want nothing to do with us. These types of things don't always turn out hunky-dory."

"I know, but after being around J.D and seeing how lost he is from not being able to remember his family, it's hard for me not to consider how important family is."

"Does that mean you're okay with what Dad did, too?"

Jenna scowled. "Hell, no. That's a whole other matter." Even if J.D. thought otherwise. "Dad created this mess."

Donna blew out her breath. "I'm glad you haven't gone completely over to the dark side."

Jenna found herself saying, "You know it's possible that Savannah isn't the hussy I've been assuming that she was. Dad could have seduced her into being with him. He could have taken advantage of her. You know how brazen he can be when he wants something."

Donna didn't disagree. But she didn't say that she was cutting Savannah any slack, either.

Jenna asked Tammy, "How do you think your brothers will vote?"

"I don't know. We'll just have to wait and see." Tammy's cell phone rang from her purse and she reached in and grabbed it. Obviously it was Doc. She all but glowed when she answered the summons. She got up and walked away to talk to him, waving goodbye to Donna and Jenna, and leaving them alone.

Neither said a word. The impending vote was only two days away, but the results, whatever they turned out to be, would last a lifetime.

Jenna arrived on J.D.'s doorstep with a slew of luggage and a worried expression, and he got worried, too.

"What's wrong?" he asked.

"I'm getting freaked out about the vote. Tammy's brothers will be here on Wednesday."

He took her luggage and brought it inside. "You already knew they were coming sometime this week."

She followed him inside. "I know. But now it seems so final."

"Are you sure you're not freaked out about *this*?" He motioned to the air between them. "About staying with me?"

"Why? Are you freaked out about it?"

"No." But he feared that he might have pushed the boundaries of their relationship, drawing her into something she couldn't handle.

"I want to stay with you. In fact, I think it's going to be a relief getting away from the main house for a while."

"So it's really the vote that's bothering you?"

She nodded. "If we search for Savannah, we'll know for sure if we have a brother or sister or cousin. And if we don't, I'll always be left wondering."

"So what are you going to do?"

"Vote yes."

He knew she'd been considering it, but she looked as if she'd just made up her mind for certain. "You'll be doing the right thing."

"Tammy is voting yes, too. But I think Donna is going to vote no."

"What about Tammy's brothers?"

"Tammy doesn't know."

They sat on the sofa together. "Does it have to be unanimous? Because if it does, it sounds like you're going to be deadlocked, regardless of how Tammy's brothers vote."

"We already agreed that the majority will rule."

"Then it still has a shot of going through."

"I hope so. Because I want to talk to Savannah and hear her side of what happened all those years ago."

"You're willing to hear her side, but not your dad's? He's the man who raised you. Who fed you and clothed you. Savannah is a stranger."

"Yes, he's the man who did all of that. But he's also the guy who turned Donna and me into the basket cases that we are."

He couldn't believe what he was hearing. "I barely know your sister, other than what you've told me about her, but from what I can tell, she isn't a basket case, and by God, neither are you. You're beautiful, hard-working, independent women. And if your dad helped shape you into those things, then he must have done something right."

She put her head on his shoulder. "Okay so maybe we're not basket cases. But we're not totally normal, either. Me with the husband checklist, and her with the inability to get close to people."

"Does this mean that you're giving up the list?"

She sat forward and laughed. "No."

He laughed, too. "Then why are you beating yourself up about it?"

"I guess I shouldn't be. Because someday the man from my list is going to appear, and I'll be living my dream life."

"As opposed to living with me in the dream cabin? You keep talking like that and you're going to make me jealous of this guy you're going to marry."

She searched his gaze. "Are you being serious?"

Was he? J.D. wasn't sure. But he said, "No. I was just goofing around."

"I should have known better than to think you would be jealous."

"I'm all for you marrying someone else."

"Stop rubbing it in."

"I'm not rubbing it in, I'm being supportive."

"If you say so."

Before it turned into an argument, he said, "Why don't we settle this with a kiss?"

"I'd rather settle it with some butterscotch pudding. Do you still have some of those?"

"Yes." But it stung that she'd avoided kissing him. "I'll get you one." He went into the kitchen and returned with the pudding and a spoon.

"Thanks." She peeled the top off the container and proceeded to eat her favorite treat.

J.D. watched her. "Can I kiss you after you're done?"

Her lips curved into a smile. "Only if you admit

that you're a little jealous of the prince who is going to marry me."

"The prince? Is that one of his requirements?"

"No. I was just being smart." She finished the pudding and set it aside. "You can kiss me if you want."

He put a hand on his heart, like a knight in a melodrama. "But I haven't sworn my jealousy yet."

"Now who's being smart?"

"Me. But I think maybe I am a little jealous. It's not that I want to be married." He sucked in his breath. "The idea of marriage still makes me panicky. But envisioning you with another man is a tough pill to swallow. Especially when I hear the way you talk about him."

"You've known from the beginning how important a husband is to me. But I'm glad you're jealous. It's better than you not caring."

"I do care. You're my lover and my friend. And I'm going to kiss you right proper. Naked and in bed."

He scooped her up and made her squeal. After carrying her to the bedroom, he plunked her down on the feather mattress, and she sank into it.

She grinned up at him. "Wow. This is comfy."

"I told you." He fell into bed with her. "I wonder if you're going to dream while you're here."

"My only dream is to be married someday, and I already know that's going to happen."

"Your list is your magic."

"I never thought of it that way before." She gazed into his eyes. "Thank you for saying that."

"What are friends for?" Immersed in her nearness, he peeled off her blouse and unhooked her bra. She in turn popped open the snaps on his shirt.

They removed the rest of their clothes and enjoyed

the luxury of bared bodies. He inhaled the fragrance of her skin, and she roamed her hands over his.

The foreplay continued until he couldn't take another minute of not having her. He opened the nightstand drawer. It was time for him to glove up, as the saying went. "I put all of the protection in here."

She peered inside. "Good thinking."

"I wanted to be prepared for you."

"You always are."

Yes, but someday he wouldn't be. Someday she would belong to someone else. Forcing his thoughts in a different direction, he said, "Tell me your most romantic fantasy."

"Besides flower petals in my honeymoon bed?"

"Yes, something besides that." He didn't want to think about her wedding night.

"Sometimes I imagine messing around in a barn."

He entered her, surrounding himself with her warmth. "You mean making love in an empty stall? We could sneak out one night and do that."

She arched her hips. "What if we got caught?"

"We'd be careful that no one else is around." He twined a finger around one of her wavy tendrils. "I'd like to see you with hay in your hair."

"I won't get hay in my hair if we bring a blanket with us."

"You will if we roll off the blanket." To show her how it might feel, he rolled over the bed, making the covers tangle. "So, what do you say, should we slip out to the barn one night?"

"And embark on my fantasy?"

"It's *our* fantasy now."

"Living with you is going to be fun."

"That's the idea." *Fun,* he thought. *Free.* But in spite of that, he kept a dangerously possessive hold on her.

After their lovemaking ended, they broke apart, but it wasn't long before they were locked in each other's arms once again.

For now, J.D. just couldn't seem to let go.

Chapter Ten

On Wednesday afternoon, Jenna, Donna and Tammy gathered on the porch of the main house with Tammy's brothers.

The women were seated in scattered chairs, and the men stood against the railing. Aidan, the older of the two, frowned and turned away from the sun, adjusting the brim of his hat. Jenna didn't know him very well, but if she had to describe him, she'd say he was the strong, silent type. Nathan was just the opposite. Already he'd been cracking silly jokes, even in the midst of turmoil.

Jenna glanced at Tammy. She looked so tiny next to her brothers. But she was also the most genuinely relaxed of anyone here. Jenna could barely breathe. Donna wasn't in any better shape. She had her hands clasped tightly on her lap.

On a side table was a pitcher of iced tea and plastic tumblers that no one had touched. The lovely new porch swing was vacant, too, creaking softly from the wind and haunting the moment.

"Does anyone want to discuss this before we get started?" Tammy asked.

"Haven't we talked enough about it already?" Donna replied. "It's been consuming our lives."

That was true, Jenna thought. They were mired in it. She'd even skipped breakfast this morning, too anxious to eat. Soon it would be time for lunch, and her stomach would be growling like a junkyard dog.

Tammy replied, "We haven't discussed it at length with Aidan and Nathan."

Her brothers exchanged a glance. Was that good or bad? Jenna wondered.

"We talked amongst ourselves," Aidan said.

"You can share your thoughts with us," Tammy said.

"What for? This isn't a jury trial. We don't have to deliberate."

"I was just giving you a chance to speak your piece."

"We'll pass," Nathan said. "But thanks all the same, Tam-boy."

Tammy didn't flinch at the childhood nickname, but he'd said it affectionately. Besides, it was obvious that she wasn't a tomboy anymore. Then again, maybe she was. Maybe it would always be part of who she was—the old Tammy blending with the new.

Jenna glanced in the direction of the stables, where J.D. was working today. He'd wished her luck before she'd left the cabin, supporting her like the true friend he was. He was a prime example of an old/new person, except that he was still in the process of remembering his old self.

"Let's do this," Aidan said, cutting through the quiet.

Tammy volunteered to go first. "My vote is yes. I think we should hire the P.I."

No one reacted, but everyone already knew what her preference was.

"Who wants to be next?" she asked.

"I'll go." Jenna figured another yes was in order. "I'm in favor, too."

The men exchanged one of those private glances again. Had they been expecting Jenna to go the other way? Or had they guessed her right? It was obvious they'd tried to peg the women's votes ahead of time.

"How about you?" Nathan asked Donna.

"I'll wait until you boys have your say."

"All right. Then it's a no for me," Nathan said.

His brother concurred. "Also a no."

Jenna's heart sank. Donna was the tiebreaker, and that meant it was a lost cause. Clearly, she was going to side with the men.

"Come on, Donna," Nathan said. "Do us proud."

But instead of complying, she got up and poured herself a glass of tea. "I need to wet my whistle first."

Nathan chuffed. "And here I thought New Yorkers did everything fast."

Donna didn't falter. "A lady has the right to weigh her options."

Jenna's pulse pounded. Was her sister actually mulling it over at the last minute or just getting everyone's goat?

As she sipped her tea like a Southern belle, Nathan muttered, "Fiddle dee dee."

Tammy cracked a smile. Jenna thought it was funny, too, but she was too nervous to smile.

The wait continued.

Then Donna turned to Jenna. "I'm doing this for you, so remember that when Savannah hates us for invading her privacy or we end up butting heads with her disgruntled kid. If there is a kid," she concluded.

Jenna grinned. No matter what the future held, she adored her sister for thinking of her. "Okay."

The tiebreaker addressed the entire group. "Just to be clear, my vote is yes."

Aidan scowled. "You certainly had us fooled. We were sure that you were going to say no."

"I was. But women are notorious for changing their minds."

"Three to two," Tammy said. "The ayes have it."

Jenna's grin widened. "Who should we hire?"

Tammy had a ready answer. "How about Roland Walker? He's the P.I. Tex used to keep an eye on all of us, so he's already familiar with our family. I think it would be easier than bringing in someone new."

"Sure. Why not?" This from Donna. "Let's keep our scandals under one roof." She laughed a little. "And use the guy who knows how screwed up the Byrds are."

Everyone else laughed, too, even Aidan, which was saying a lot.

Soon the men went into the house, and Tammy followed them, giving the sisters a moment to themselves.

"Thank you," Jenna said. "What you did means everything to me."

"I knew how important it was to you. But I hope it doesn't come back to bite us in the butt."

"I don't think it will. But even if it does, I'll never forget that you sacrificed your vote for mine."

They got out of their chairs, and Jenna reached out to hug her selfless sibling. She couldn't remember the last time she hugged Donna.

But it felt incredible.

J.D. glanced up and saw Jenna rushing toward him with exuberance. He struggled to collect his wits, preparing to greet her.

His day had started off fine, but as it wore on, dark and disturbing feelings had begun coming over him. And now here he was, trapped in the ache of a family he couldn't remember. But it wasn't just a case of not remembering them; he'd been dealing with that all along. It was the foreboding sense that whatever had gone wrong in his family couldn't be fixed.

As Jenna approached him, he slapped a smile on his face. He wasn't about to drag her down with his discomfort.

"It went well, I take it?" he asked.

"You wouldn't believe how well."

While she chattered about the outcome, giving him the details, he stood beside the barn, wearing damp jeans and a pair of rubber boots. Aside from having troublesome thoughts for the last few hours, he'd been bathing horses.

"Can you believe it?" she said. "Donna voted yes for me."

He'd never seen her so energized. If he wasn't so dirty and sweaty, and if his emotions weren't teetering on a thread, he would've lifted her off the ground and given her a little twirl. "I'm glad it worked out for you."

"It more than worked out. This mess with Savannah brought Donna and me closer. And you should have seen how funny she made it all seem. She had everyone laughing by the time it was over, and Aidan doesn't laugh that easily."

It was obvious how proud she was of her sister, and how much love there really was between them.

Jenna kept chattering. "We agreed to use the P.I. Tex had used. He must be good or Tex wouldn't have hired him. I'll bet he locates Savannah in no time."

"You have hope."

"Yes, I do. Donna warned me that it could turn out badly, but I don't think it will. I told her that it didn't matter, though, because what's most important is what she did for me."

"Happiness looks good on you."

"Thank you." She took a moment to catch her breath. "So how's your day going?"

The question hit him like the recoil from a high-powered rifle, nearly knocking the truth out of him. But he said, "Fine," determined not to spoil her mood.

Her stomach growled, and she laughed. "I knew that was going to happen. I still haven't eaten today."

"Then go get something."

"I will. And then you know what I'm going to do? I'm going to ask Tammy if she'll give me a cooking lesson."

"So you can feed your future husband?"

"Yes, but so I can make dinner sometime for you, too. You've been offering to be my guinea pig. You're still willing, aren't you?"

He nodded. "You can cook for me anytime you want."

"What should I focus on? What type of meal?"

"It doesn't matter."

"Of course it does. I want to learn to make your favorite food." She cocked her head. "Do you have a favorite that you're aware of? Or something you recently acquired a taste for?"

He roamed his gaze over her, pushing his bad feelings aside. "The only recent taste I acquired is for you."

She blushed. "I'm being serious, J.D."

So was he.

"There must be something you favor."

"I'm partial to Japanese food." The information zoomed right out, without him expecting it. He even jerked in surprise.

So did Jenna. "Oh, wow. Did you just remember that?"

"Yes." But he didn't have a clue why it was his food of choice. All he knew was that it was.

"That's so cool." She smiled at his horse-washing attire. "A sushi cowboy. Who would have guessed?"

Certainly not him.

She said, "As much as I'd like to accommodate your selection, I think Japanese might be a bit too ambitious for me to try. I doubt Tammy cooks in that style, either. Anything else?"

He gave her the option of choosing. "What's your favorite food? Or better yet, what do you want to learn to make? What do you see yourself cooking?"

She concentrated on the question. "Mom used to make spaghetti and meatballs, and sometimes I used to sing that silly parody of 'Old Smoky.'"

"The one where the meatball rolls on to the ground when somebody sneezed?"

She grinned. "Yep."

He grinned, too. She was improving his day, minute by confusing minute. "Now that I'd like to see."

"Me singing the song or the meatball rolling on to the ground?"

He chuckled. "Both."

"Here's an idea. I can turn my lesson into a family dinner. Tammy and I can fix the food, and maybe Donna, too, and you, Doc, Aidan and Nathan can hang out with us. Then, when it's ready, everyone can eat."

"Sounds great."

"I'm going to give the household staff the night off. I want to keep this low-key, without anyone else around, except the Savannah voters and our significant others."

He didn't deny that he was her significant other. Temporary as their agreement was, he still fit the bill. "I'll be there." And hopefully without a dark cloud hovering over his head.

Hours later, J.D. assessed the flock in the kitchen. By definition, "flock" meant a number of birds feeding, resting or traveling together, and these Byrds intended to eat together this evening.

And eat hearty.

The upcoming menu consisted of the aforementioned spaghetti and meatballs, along with deep-fried zucchini, garlic bread and a big green salad. For dessert—ice cream and fresh berries.

Jenna's lesson was a time-consuming project. To keep the masses from going hungry, Tammy had prepared a relish tray, and her Texas-size brothers were stuffing cold meats and cheeses in their mouths.

Nathan, the more talkative of the two, asked J.D.,

"So, who are you, exactly? Besides the guy who lost his memory? What's your role around here?"

"I work on the Flying B. I'm dating Jenna, too. She's staying with me in the dream cabin."

"You mean Savannah's old cabin? Maybe it should be called the nightmare cabin, considering everything that went on."

"Hey," Doc interjected. "That cabin helped me win my girl."

Tammy sent her fiancé a loving look.

Nathan rolled his eyes and spoke to Jenna. "You're the slowest cook I've ever seen. Isn't that a device of some kind? A slow cooker? Maybe that should be your ranch nickname." He cocked a gunslinger stance. "Slow Cooker, the pokiest chef in the West."

"Shut up, you big brute." She threw a dish towel at her jokester cousin, but missed him by a mile.

The Slow Cooker handle isn't half bad, J.D. thought. Jenna had only made two or three meatballs compared to the dozens Tammy had made. But J.D. thought Jenna looked damned cute doing it.

"I hope you don't plan on marrying her," Nathan said. "You'll starve."

Oh, cripes. J.D. didn't know how to react or how to respond. He certainly couldn't tell the other man how many marriage discussions he and Jenna had engaged in, but with a different groom in mind. Clearly Jenna wasn't going to say it, either.

Tammy came to the rescue. "Nobody is getting married, except Mike and me."

Nathan went with the flow. "Yep, my baby sister nabbed a doctor, and a damned fine one."

"Thanks," Doc said.

"Remember I said that when you're choosing your best man." Nathan grinned, then gauged the activity, his gaze landing on Donna and Aidan, who'd been staying quiet. "You know what this party needs? Some vino from Tex's cellar."

Aidan finally spoke up. "We're having Chianti with dinner."

"I know, but it'll be forever before we eat. I think we need to get buzzed now. Allow me to do the honors."

After he left to pilfer the spirits, Aidan said to J.D., "Sometimes my brother is full of himself. I hope he isn't offending you."

"None taken. But thank you."

Nathan returned with two bottles. He read from the first label. "This lovely vintage is a Montepulciana." He did the same thing with the second one. "And this robust selection is a Barbera." He dropped the act and grinned. "Mix your reds, I always say."

"That's because you don't know anything about wine," his brother commented.

"I know enough to enjoy them." He popped open the corks and poured everyone a drink, whether they wanted one or not. "How about a little music?" He turned on the radio and scanned the dial until he found a song that amused him.

He extended a hand to Donna, trying to persuade her to dance to Billy Ray Cyrus's anthem with him.

She rebuffed his attempt to make a Buckshot Hills filly out of her, shooing him away to "Achy Breaky" with someone else.

Nathan waggled his eyebrows at his brother.

"Me?" Aidan shook his head. "Get real."

The carefree Byrd danced by himself, creating

an imaginary partner and swinging her around. Doc grinned and swept Tammy into his arms. When Jenna looked expectantly at J.D., he went for it, too. He led her into a two-step, and they laughed while they rocked to the rowdy beat.

The partnering didn't last long. Nathan started a line dance, and the rest of them followed. Even Aidan jumped in, kicking up his heels.

But not Donna. She darted over to the stove, as if she was saving the food from Billy Ray's old mullet.

"That one needs some country spirit," Nathan said. "Too bad there isn't a guy around to upset her Big City Apple cart."

Jenna and Tammy exchanged a behind-the-scenes glance, and J.D. assumed that they were thinking about Caleb Granger and his supposed attraction to Donna. But neither woman said anything to Nathan. Obviously they didn't trust him not to create a scene over it. Besides, Caleb was still out of town, and from what J.D. had heard about him from Manny, Caleb was a player with tons of women at his disposal. Donna didn't need her cart upset quite that far.

Soon the line dancers disbursed. Jenna and Tammy joined Donna at the stove, and the brothers went outside to grab some air.

Doc came over to J.D. and put his hand on his shoulder. "Tammy told me how your memory is starting to return. I'm glad you recalled some good things about yourself."

Good things. Doc was obviously referring to the Sam Houston/Cherokee information. J.D. wanted to tell him about the dark feelings he'd been dealing with today, but now wasn't the time. So he simply said, "Thanks."

"We'll miss you around here when you're gone."

"I'll miss this crazy clan, too." But mostly he would miss Jenna. As she bustled around the kitchen, barely getting anything done, he thought about the man she was going to marry. Whoever he was, he would be a lucky guy.

Overall, the dinner was a success. The meal was delicious, and Jenna seemed proud of her Slow Cooker accomplishments. The newly formed group ate in the formal dining room, with a linen tablecloth, polished silverware and a floral centerpiece. *The Byrds,* J.D. thought as he glanced around at their faces.

A wonderfully mixed-up flock learning to be a family.

Chapter Eleven

The following morning at the cabin, J.D. and Jenna had breakfast—toaster waffles, doused in maple syrup.

She said, "I wonder if my next lesson should be waffles. Or do you like pancakes better?"

"I like either one." But mostly he liked her. She still had the same sunny disposition from yesterday. And he'd yet to tell her what was going on with him.

"Do you think it's the same batter?"

"What?"

"Pancakes and waffles?"

"I don't know."

"I'll have to talk to Tammy about it. She makes this really good chicken and waffles dish."

Barely hearing her, J.D. gazed at the clouds in his coffee.

"What's wrong? You seem preoccupied."

He glanced up. "I've been having bad feelings about my past."

She put down her fork. "What do you mean?"

He stopped eating, too. "I'm certain that whatever went wrong in my family can't be repaired."

"How can you be certain of something like that?"

"It's just what I feel, what I sense." Deep inside, where it counted.

"Do you have any memories to go along with those feelings?"

"No."

"Then I don't understand your certainty. You could be confused." She continued to evaluate the unknown situation. "What sort of thing could have happened that can't be repaired? Look at what's going on in my family and how we're coping with it."

"You haven't forgiven your dad."

"That's different."

"What makes your family different from mine?"

She clammed up.

"See," he said. "No difference."

"If I reached out to my dad, would you change your perspective about your family? Would you start to believe that whatever went wrong could be repaired?"

"I can't make a judgment call like that until I remember my past."

"We could hire Roland Walker to try to find out who you are. He would have a lot more time to devote to your case than the police."

He shook his head. "I appreciate the suggestion, but I'd rather let the sheriff's department handle it. Or better yet, to remember on my own."

"But you haven't remembered yet, and a P.I. would

delve deeper than the police. All they're doing is trying to find out your name and if you were carjacked."

"And that's exactly why I don't want Roland involved. I'm not comfortable with someone digging up bones."

"Does Doc know that you're having bad feelings?"

"I wanted to tell him last night, but it wasn't the right time."

"Would you mind if we talked to him together?"

"Not at all. In fact, I would prefer it." At this stage, he wanted to be as truthful as possible and for Jenna to know him as well as he knew himself, which wasn't saying much, he supposed. But it was the best he could do. "I'm not trying to hide anything from you. I think it's important to be honest. Otherwise our affair wouldn't seem right."

"Honesty is the very first quality on my list."

The vast blueness of her eyes nearly pulled him under, but her comment had packed an even bigger punch.

So much so, it became overly apparent.

"I'm sorry," she stammered. "I didn't mean to imply that you…"

He almost wished that she was, but it was wrong for him to feel that way, especially amid the murky waters in his mind. "I didn't think you were. We both know I'm not the guy from your list."

She went silent, and he studied her, intrigued by the way daylight zigzagged through the blinds and cast a glow on her hair. But there were always little things about her that fascinated him.

Interrupting the quiet, she picked up her fork. He resumed eating, as well.

She said, "I wonder if you're going to have any more dreams while you're here. Or if your memories will return while you're awake."

"If my memories are bad, I hope they don't come in dreams. Because if they did, then Nathan would be right. This would be the nightmare cabin."

"That would be awful."

He nodded, then asked, "Are you ever going to reach out to your dad?"

"I would if it would help you come to terms with your family and whatever is causing the darkness."

"You can't fix me, Jenna. You can only fix what's broken within yourself."

"I know. But I want to make you feel better."

"You are. Believe me. Just knowing that you care matters."

"Same goes for me."

Before it got too emotional, he said, "We better finish up and get to work."

"When should we talk to Doc?"

"Tonight, if he's around."

They cleared the table and left the cabin. They walked to the stables together, then went their separate ways. He rode fence with Hugh, and she went into the barn to tend to her horses. And although J.D. was swamped with work, he thought about Jenna throughout the day and suspected that she was thinking of him, too.

Doc stopped by the cabin that evening, and Jenna listened while he and J.D. talked.

"Do you think my mind is playing tricks on me?" J.D. asked.

"Do you think that's what is happening?" the other man asked in return.

"No, but Jenna mentioned it."

Doc didn't ask her to expound on her opinion, but there was no need. It was obvious that she was troubled by J.D having a past that couldn't be repaired. Or a past that he didn't *think* could be repaired. There was a difference. She knew that better than anyone, and it was starting to make her guilty for hanging on to her Daddy resentments.

J.D. spoke to Doc again. "Jenna suggested hiring Roland Walker to hunt down my identity, but I don't want to do that. It's too personal to bring a P.I. into it."

"I understand," came the professional reply. "Another option would be to talk to a psychologist. I can recommend someone, if you'd like."

"Why do I need to talk to someone else? I'm already talking to you."

"This isn't my field of expertise, J.D."

"But I'm comfortable with you."

"Then you can continue to confide in me. I want to help in any way I can."

"Give me your opinion. I want to know what you think, regardless of your field of expertise."

"All right." Doc's voice was strong and steady, like the man he was. "I think that you need to relax and not worry so much about it. It seems obvious, to me anyway, that you need more time to address your feelings. And I think your memories will become clear when your mind is able to process the past and accept it, whatever it entails."

It was good advice, Jenna thought, and made complete sense to her.

"That's pretty much what you told me in the beginning," J.D. said. "To relax and let things happen naturally."

"And it still applies."

"I've had uneasy feelings about myself from the start, but it's getting harder to handle now that they're progressing."

"But what about the positive things you've recalled? It's not all bad."

J.D. furrowed his brows. "Meaning what? That every cloud has a silver lining, even the stormy ones?"

"I'd certainly like to think so."

"Ditto," Jenna said.

J.D. shook his head. "There you go ganging up on me. You two did that at the hospital, convincing me to stay here."

"That didn't turn out so badly, did it?" Doc asked.

J.D.'s expression softened, and when he glanced at Jenna, her heart went sweet and gooey.

"It turned out really nice," he said, still looking at her.

Her heart went even gooier. She was working so incredibly hard *not* to fall in love with him, and at this point, all she could do was keep praying that she didn't melt at his feet.

J.D. continued to look at her. She wanted him to break eye contact, but at the same time, she wanted to freeze this moment and keep it forever.

Forever. A dangerous word. A dangerous wish.

On and on it went. The look. The emotional push-pull. The fear of falling in love with him.

Then, thankfully, Doc cleared his throat, snaring J.D.'s attention and making Jenna breathe easier.

J.D. said to Doc, "I'll keep your advice in mind."

"Just let me know any time you need to talk."

"Thanks. I appreciate it."

Both men stood up and shook hands. Jenna got to her feet, too. Doc smiled at her, and she suspected it was his way of trying to help her relax. No doubt he could tell that she was fighting her feelings for J.D.

After Tammy's fiancé left, Jenna went into the kitchen to heat a pan of milk, her way of dealing with her feelings.

"Are you making hot chocolate?" J.D. asked.

"No. Just the milk. I can make hot chocolate for you, though."

"That's okay. I don't want anything." He leaned against the counter. "Remember when I made tea for you at the motel?"

She nodded.

"I think it was because I used to know someone who drank tea. Someone I was close to."

She started. "A former lover?"

"I don't know. It was a random feeling." He motioned to the pan she'd put on the stove. "I prefer cold milk."

"I like it cold, too. But Mom used to warm it for me when I was a kid. It's a comfort thing."

"That's nice." He came forward and slipped his arms around her. "You know what gives me comfort? Being around you."

She returned his hug, breathing in his masculine beauty and keeping him close. "What am I going to do after you're gone?"

"Find the man of your dreams," he whispered.

The man of my dreams, she thought. The man she

loved. That was a lost cause. Because deep down, she knew that she'd already found him.

The week passed without incident. Roland Walker hadn't located Savannah yet or uncovered anything about her that indicated whether she'd had a child, J.D. hadn't remembered anything new about himself and Jenna was still struggling with the revelation that she loved him.

And now as she prepared to meet J.D. on their break, her pulse wouldn't stop pounding.

She removed their sack lunches from the fridge in the barn and headed to the spot they'd agreed upon, just east of the stables and beneath a shady tree.

Plunking down beneath the towering oak, she waited for him.

He arrived shortly, and as he walked toward her, he looked sinfully sexy, moving with a long, lean gait. He also had Tex's borrowed Stetson perched low on his head. Jenna was wearing a hat, too, with a red bandana tied around the outside of the crown.

"Afternoon," he said, and sat in the grass next to her.

She handed him his lunch, as nervous as a calf in the midst of being roped. Only it was her heart that was being lassoed.

"Are you okay?" he asked, obviously noticing that she seemed off. "Did something happen with Savannah?"

"No." Being honest about what was bothering her wasn't something she was capable of doing, not without admitting that she loved him. So she tried to wrangle in her emotions or at least not let them show. "There's no news. And I'm fine. Just hungry." She opened her sack and removed her sandwich, forcing a bite.

He didn't eat right away. Instead, he took a drink of his water. She watched him swallow, fascinated by the line of his neck and the way his Adam's apple bobbed with the effort.

"You were staring at me," he said afterward.

"Was I?"

"Uh-huh."

"Turnabout is fair play. You stare at me all the time, too."

"Guilty as charged. But neither of us should be doing it."

"Because it isn't polite to stare?"

"Yep." He leaned over and kissed her.

Heavens, he was the best kisser in the world. She wanted to crawl on to his lap and rub herself all over him, like a cat in heat. Or a woman in the throes of love.

"You taste like roast beef and avocado." He grinned. "Tastes good."

"I packed you the same lunch." She gestured to his sack. "Go for it."

"Don't mind if I do." He unwrapped his sandwich. "You're getting better at the kitchen stuff."

Wife practice, she thought, with a man who would never be her husband. "I'm trying."

He gazed at the bandana tied around her hat. Then blinked in an interested way.

"What?" she asked.

"The color just made me think of something. On the Native American medicine wheel, red symbolizes success and triumph."

"You just had another Cherokee memory."

"Apparently so." He sounded pleased. "And your hatband was the trigger."

She wasn't feeling triumphant or successful. But she summoned a smile, for his sake. "That's nice, J.D."

"It's a lot better than those dark feelings."

"Are you still having those?"

"Yes." They sat quietly and ate, then he said, "I hope this isn't going to sound like a loaded question, but how do you feel about the Savannah situation now that you're interested in meeting her? Do you want there to be another Byrd? Or would you prefer that there is no child?"

It *was* a loaded question, and she considered it carefully. "If there is no child, it will be a relief not to have to worry about who that person is and how he or she will fit into our lives. But on the other hand, if there isn't, I might actually be disappointed. Like I lost someone in my family that I never even got to know."

"I would feel that way, too." He glanced away and frowned.

Really, really frowned, she noticed.

"Did you just remember something bad?" she asked, analyzing how quickly his mood had changed.

"The children." He stared straight ahead. "I remember them. Or sort of remember…"

She leaned toward him. "What children?"

He discarded his lunch, crinkling the bag in his distress. "There were kids in my family who got left behind. I don't know who they were or how many of them there were, but I can feel their existence."

"What do you mean? Left behind?"

"In foster care. Kids who were supposed to get adopted but never were. That's why I know about the foster-care system. That's why it's been so important to me."

Her heart dropped to her stomach. Was it possible that they were his kids? That he was their biological father? Or that he'd actually been married? Was that why the thought of having a wife and kids made him panic?

No, she thought. He was too kind, too decent to have given up on his children or let them be taken away from him. And with the recurring talk of marriage, with it being a constant topic, wouldn't he have remembered having a wife, especially now with the foster-children memory?

"Was it you?" she asked, just to see what he would say.

He blinked. "What?"

"Did you father them?"

"No. God, no. I wasn't their dad."

"Are you sure?"

"Yes. I'm absolutely certain that I've never been a parent."

She gladly accepted his response, grateful that his feelings were so strong in that regard. "I didn't think you were, but I thought I should mention it, in case it was possible."

He was still frowning, still visibly troubled. "I don't know whose kids they were, but losing them is part of the darkness. Of what went wrong in my family and why it can't be fixed." He paused. "Doc said that I would remember things when I can handle it. But I don't want to remember anything else. Not today."

"Then don't think about it anymore."

"I'm not going to. It makes my head hurt."

It made his heart hurt, too, she thought, feeling sad

for him. She wanted him to have a bright and happy future. She wanted that for herself, too.

And their families.

After work, Jenna thought long and hard about what she needed to do, and when she came to a decision, she told J.D. that she was going to go for a walk with her sister. But she didn't tell him why she'd summoned Donna. She didn't tell Donna, either.

So, as the women strolled along the ranch, a soft hush drifted between them.

"What's going on?" her sister finally asked.

"I have something important to talk to you about."

Donna stopped walking. Jenna did, too, and with the sun setting in the sky, she said, "I'm going to go see Dad on Saturday, and I'm going to ask him to tell me why he betrayed Uncle William and slept with Savannah. And no matter his excuse, I'm going to do my damnedest to forgive him."

Her sister took a step back, and a twig snapped beneath her shiny black boot. "Just like that? You're going to let him off the hook?"

"I'm in love with J.D."

Donna flinched in surprise or maybe it was confusion or both. "What does one have to do with the other?"

"J.D. has been saying that there are things in his family that can't be fixed, and now he's starting to remember some of those issues."

"So you're going to try to fix the way you feel about Dad? How is that going to help J.D.?"

"It isn't. But it's going to help me comes to terms with what Dad did. And hopefully it will help Dad in some way, too."

"Please don't ask me to go with you. I'm not ready to see him."

"I know you're not. I also know that this is more difficult for you than it is for me. I was always disappointed in him, but you used to idolize him."

The city girl set her jaw. "I did not."

"Say what you will, but I used to see the way you looked at him. You aspired to be like him. He was strong and tough, and he was your role model. I never expected much of him, but you did. And he let you down."

Donna took another step back, and Jenna thought her big sis looked like she was ready to bolt, to run straight back to New York as swiftly as her long, gorgeous legs would take her.

Then Donna said, "I don't want to have this conversation with you."

"Yes, I can see that." Hence, Jenna wasn't going to push it. "I just wanted you to know that I was driving to Houston on Saturday."

"Don't give Dad my regards."

"I won't."

Donna turned and walked away, but she didn't go far. She came back with a concerned expression. "Does J.D. know that you love him?"

"No."

"Are you going to tell him?"

Her heart clenched. "No."

"Why not?"

"Because it won't change anything. And because I wasn't supposed to get attached. He and I talked about it ahead of time, and I kept insisting that I wouldn't."

"I'm sorry if you're hurting."

"Thank you." She longed to hug Donna the way she'd

done on the day of the vote, but she feared that she might cry in her sister's arms. And that wouldn't do either of them any good.

They parted company, and Jenna continued to walk by herself, immersed in her surroundings. The Flying B was her home, the place that gave her hope, but would it be enough to sustain her after J.D. was gone?

She thought about Tammy and Doc and how lucky Tammy was. Her cousin had the ranch, but she had the man she loved, too. What if Jenna never found anyone to replace J.D.? What if she compared every man she met to him—to his qualities—instead of what was on her list?

Maybe she should throw that stupid list away.

She frowned at the path in front of her. She couldn't do it. She'd compiled it for a reason, and she was keeping it, especially since J.D had told her it was her magic.

Her magic. Her pain. Her confusion.

Before her emotions drove her straight into a ditch, she headed for the cabin, where she knew J.D. would be awaiting her return.

She went inside and came face-to-face with her lover, who was fresh from his evening shower and attired in a plain white T-shirt and crisply laundered jeans.

"How was your walk?" he asked.

She blew out the air in her lungs. "I told Donna what I needed to tell her." And now it was time to tell him, except for the part about loving him, of course. "I'm going to my dad's on Saturday."

"You are?" He widened his eyes. "To try to square things with him?"

She nodded. "What you recalled about your family

has made me think deeper about mine. I can't keep letting my wound fester. I have to find a way to heal it."

"I'm so proud of you and the progress you've made." He took her in his arms. "Knowing that you're going to be okay will make my leaving easier when the time comes."

She buried her cheek against his neck, her emotions going haywire again. "What if I'm not okay? What if I turn into a lonely old spinster, waiting for a man who never appears?"

"Are you kidding? Your future husband is out there and he's going to be everything you imagined."

She buried her face deeper into the warmth of his skin. "Are you still jealous of him?"

"Hell, yes. But I'm glad he exists, too. That he'll be there when you need him."

What she needed was for him to be J.D., not a nameless, faceless stranger.

He said, "Someday you're going to get married with your entire family in attendance, and it will be the best day of your life."

How could it be the best day of her life unless she was marrying him? "I don't want to think about my wedding right now." Unable to let go, she clung to him, like a love-fraught reed in the wind. "I just need to deal with going to Houston on Saturday."

And the reconciliation with her father.

Chapter Twelve

As Jenna parked her truck and took in her surroundings, the familiar blue-and-white house stirred pangs of loneliness. But what did she expect, for this pristine suburban structure and its perfectly manicured lawn to give her a happy sense of home?

She would never forget the day she and Donna had moved in with their dad. They'd been two young girls raw from their mother's passing, and the ache was as vivid today as it had been then.

She exited her vehicle, her mind alive with deathly memories. The friends and neighbors who'd brought casseroles by had meant well, but their condolences hadn't helped. Dad, Donna and Jenna had made an awkward trio. The divorced father with his motherless children. The busy executive who'd been estranged from his own family. They'd been doomed from the start.

Jenna moved forward, taking the shrub-lined walkway toward the front door. She'd called ahead and let Dad know that she was coming, only now that she was here, she wanted to turn tail and run. But she quickened her pace and approached the awning-covered stoop. She no longer had a key. She'd gotten her own apartment ages ago, and now, of course, she was living at the Flying B.

She rang the bell, and Dad opened the door, appearing like a cautious mirage. They gazed uncomfortably at each other. He was an attractive man for his age, with striking blue eyes and graying brown hair. He stayed in shape by hitting the gym. His only lazy indulgence was the TV game show that he plunked himself in front of each night.

She went inside. He kept the place tidy, especially for a bachelor, but it lacked warmth. It had been that way ever since she was a child. Something had always been missing.

"Do you want a cola?" he asked.

She shook her head. He kept pop around for guests, but he rarely entertained. She couldn't actually remember him dating anyone, either. If he had lovers, he never brought them home for her and Donna to see.

He spoke again. "Where do you want to sit?"

"The living room is fine."

He offered her the sofa. "I'm not much of a talker, Jenna."

"I know, Dad. But this is a discussion we need to have." She hadn't told him that she wanted to make amends. She'd just said that she wanted to discuss their family.

He sat in his easy chair, the one from which he normally watched TV, only the television was off.

She said, "I have a lot of questions about the past. But first I wanted to check to see if anyone informed you about the outcome of the vote."

"William called me and said it went through. His kids gave him the details. Tammy was in favor of hiring the P.I. and Aidan and Nathan weren't, but their votes were canceled out by yours and Donna's. So now Roland Walker is searching for Savannah."

That pretty much summed it up. "I didn't know that you and Uncle William were on speaking terms, other than snapping at each other."

"We're not. He called out of anger, to remind me of what a mess I made out of everyone's lives. How many times do I have to hear that?"

"As many times as it takes."

He heaved a heavy sigh. "So you're here to berate me, too?"

"No. Actually, I came here to forgive you, Dad."

"You could have fooled me."

She bristled. This was going to be harder than she'd thought. "Maybe I should just leave and forget it."

"No, please. Stay. I miss you and Donna." He shifted in his chair, looking big and tough and troubled. "How is your sister?"

"She's fine."

"Why didn't she come with you?"

"She isn't ready to make amends with you."

He didn't reply, but he seemed wounded. Did he know that Donna used to idolize him? Or had he been too consumed with himself all these years to notice?

Jenna hoped and prayed that forgiving him was truly

the right thing to do. Clearly he was hurting, but if it was self-indulgent pain, then it didn't count, not the way it should.

She asked, "How do you feel about us looking for Savannah and her possible child?"

He skirted the issue. "William is upset about it."

"I know. But how do *you* feel?"

He hesitated, obviously not keen about answering the question.

"Dad."

"I was in love with her, Jenna."

That was the last thing she'd expected to hear. And because it took her by complete surprise, she merely sat there, probably with a stupid look on her face.

He continued, "Out-of-my-head, out-of-my-young-heart in love. I even married your mother on the rebound because I'd lost Savannah. Your mom reminded me a bit of her, but they weren't the same woman, and I never got over Savannah. She was always there, like a ghost who wouldn't stop torturing me."

Conflicted by his admission, Jenna tensed, feeling sorry for him and hating him at the same time. "Did Mom know about Savannah?"

"No. I didn't tell her that I was estranged from my family because of a girl. I didn't make up a story, either. I just said that it was too painful to talk about, and she accepted it. I think in the beginning, my rebel-boy pain made me more appealing to your mom."

Jenna's voice went sharp. "She wouldn't have found it appealing if she'd known you were pining over another woman."

"I tried to make the marriage work. Honestly, I did.

But I didn't love your mom the way I should have, and she began to lose feelings for me, too."

"I remember Mom being distraught over the divorce."

"You were six years old when we split up. How clear can your memories be?"

Clear enough, she thought. "I remember how often she cried. And how much time she started spending at her job. She didn't seem like the same Mommy anymore." But Jenna had stayed by her side, sticking like kindergarten paste, right up until the day she'd died.

He stared at the empty TV screen. "I never meant to hurt her."

"You hurt a lot of people."

"I didn't set out to do that."

She took an enormous breath, struggling to give him the benefit of the doubt. "Tell me more about Savannah and how your relationship with her unfolded."

"William and I were both home from school that summer. Me from Rice University and him from Texas A&M. It was our first year of college. William was majoring in animal husbandry so he could work beside Tex on the ranch, and I was majoring in business with a minor in economics, so I could get the hell off the Flying B someday."

She knew some of these details already, but she'd arranged this meeting to hear his version of the story, so she listened to the way he was telling it, concentrating on the emotional inflection in his voice.

He continued, "Right before summer break, William had gotten into a car accident and ended up with a fractured leg, a sprained wrist and some cuts and bruises on his face. So that's the condition he was in when he came home. He'd been dating Savannah for a while by then. She was a student at A&M, too. Since he was all banged up, she offered to drive him to the ranch and help nurse him back to health." He paused, then added, "I arrived a few days later, and from the moment I met Savannah, I was awestruck. But I kept telling myself that I was only attracted to her because she was William's girl. I'd always felt a raging sense of competition with my brother."

She interrupted. "Why, Dad?"

"Because Tex favored him. Tex never said so, but it was obvious to me from the time we were kids. William's love of the Flying B was a bond they shared, and it alienated me from them. I fought back by competing with William. But he was just as macho as I was, and he pushed back, competing with me, too. In retrospect, I probably created that holy-hell trait in him."

"Or maybe you both inherited it from Tex. Grandpa was an ornery old guy."

"That's for damn sure. Ornery when he was old. Ornery when he was young. Our father had always been a powerful force to be reckoned with." He glanced away.

She urged him on. "Finish telling me about Savannah."

He complied. "Since William was laid up, I spent a lot of time with her, entertaining her on the ranch. The Flying B was a heck of a lot more fun with her around. We took walks, we rode trail, we picnicked by the stream."

Jenna merely nodded. She'd been doing those same activities with J.D.

"She was charming and beautiful, and I started falling in love with her. Genuinely in love. I battled with my conscience every day, trying to make my feelings stop, but I couldn't. I wanted her so damned much. Finally, I reached the point of not caring that she was William's girl."

"How did she feel about you?"

"She went mad for me, too. In fact, she'd been awestruck over me from the moment we met, just the way I was over her. It wasn't the same between her and William. They had a nice easy relationship that she'd assumed was love. Only after she met me, she knew the difference. Of course she was terribly guilty over William, too. She kept saying that she needed to break the news to him. We even discussed coming clean and telling him together. One way or another, William had to be told."

"But neither of you followed through?"

He shook his head, frowned. "Actually, we did just the opposite. We kept sleeping together. But we'd never done it at the cabin until the night we got caught. Prior to that, we'd been having secret trysts, mostly in the hills, away from the Flying B."

Jenna went quiet. At this point she didn't know what to say. But her silence wasn't a problem, because her dad kept talking, as if he needed to get the whole sordid story off his chest.

He said, "Funny thing, too, when Savannah and William first arrived, Tex had insisted that she stay in the dream cabin because it was the farthest from the house. I think it was to stop her and William from getting frisky under his roof. He hadn't counted on me being tossed into the mix."

Once again, Jenna said nothing.

He spoke further. "After Savannah and I were together that night, I snuck out of there as fast I could, and ran smack dab into Tex, who'd gone for a walk to smoke one of his fancy-ass cigars. I was in the midst of tucking in my shirt and adjusting my belt. He knew instantly what I'd been doing with Savannah in the cabin. He lit into me, calling me every rotten name in the book. According to Tex, I was the biggest SOB that ever lived and Savannah was a trollop who'd cuckolded one twin for the other. He refused to listen to anything I had to say, so I didn't even bother trying to explain myself or tell him how much Savannah and I loved each other."

She went into question mode again. "So what did you do?"

"I blasted over to the main house to pack my things. But I was planning on going back to the cabin after Tex went to bed. To ask Savannah to run away with me." He gave a long drawn-out pause. "But later, when I returned to the cabin, she was gone. I figured that Tex had given her a piece of his mind and kicked her off the ranch. I left, too, and headed for A&M, where I thought she'd gone. But she didn't return to school. She just up and disappeared, and I never saw her again."

"And you had no idea that she'd taken a pregnancy test or that she suspected that she might be pregnant?"

"No. None."

"If there is a child, do you think it's yours? Or was she sleeping with William at the same time she was with you?"

"She wasn't with us at the same time. William will confirm that he hadn't slept with her after his accident. But he'd been with her before, so if there is a child, it could still be his. She could have been pregnant when she'd come to the ranch and not even known it."

"Tell me how you feel about the possibility of Savannah having a child, Dad."

"I'm hoping that there isn't one. I can't bear the thought of her and William having a son or daughter, for his sake as much as mine. But, by the same token, I can't handle being a father again. I'm already a lousy parent to you and Donna."

She extended her heart to him. After everything he'd told her, she empathized with him now. "You did the best you could."

"Do you still think I'm a monster for having an affair with my brother's girlfriend?"

"No, but I think she should have broken it off with William first. You and Savannah should have showed more restraint."

"Being in love messes people up."

"I know," she replied, suddenly trapped in her own life, her own feelings.

His gaze zoomed in on hers, his blue eyes filled with fatherly concern. "Is there a young man I should know about?"

Unable to hold back, she nodded. Then she proceeded to tell him about J.D.

Afterward, he said, "You need to tell him that you love him."

"But I promised him that I wouldn't get attached, and he's determined to leave the ranch after his memory returns."

He got up and sat beside her. "My affair with Savannah turned into a disaster, but at least we spoke about our feelings. In that regard, I don't have any regrets."

"You're right." So very right. "If J.D. leaves the ranch

without me telling him that I love him, I'll regret that for the rest of my life."

"It's possible that he loves you, too. But he's too mixed up with his amnesia to realize it. Once his memory comes back, it might work in your favor."

"Do you really think so?"

"Truthfully, I can't imagine him *not* loving you. You're a special girl, Jenna."

She put her head on his shoulder. "Thanks, Daddy."

"You haven't called me that since you were little."

They turned to look at each other, and she smiled. "I'm glad I came here. J.D. kept telling me that I should."

"I think I'd like that boy."

"I think so, too. There's a lot to like about him."

"There was a lot to like about Savannah, too. She was a foster child, and all she ever wanted was a family. I had a tough time understanding that since I was such an outsider in mine."

"J.D. has a connection to foster kids, too. Only he isn't quite sure who they are to him." She thought about his childhood dream, about his scattered memories. "Did Savannah dream while she was at the cabin?"

"I don't know. If she did, she never mentioned it."

"I haven't dreamed while I've been there."

"Not everyone does."

They sat quietly, then she asked, "Does Uncle William know that you loved Savannah? Have you ever told him?"

"No."

"You should tell him. You should apologize to him, too."

"After all of this time? Hell, we're practically old

men now." He made a face, aging himself even more—
the lines around his eyes crinkling, his lips thinning.

"Yes, after all of this time." She reprimanded him.
"Your apology is long overdue."

"Do you know how difficult that's going to be for
me?"

"No more difficult than me telling J.D. that I love
him."

He cursed beneath his breath.

She stared him down.

"Okay." He held out his hands in surrender. "I'll go
out on a limb if you will." He lowered his hands and
gentled his voice. "It would be nice if you tried to talk
me up to your sister, too."

"I'll try." But first she was going to talk to J.D. If she
waited, she feared her nerves would explode. She gathered her purse. "I'm going to go home now."

"Call me later and tell me how it went."

"You, too."

He walked her to her truck, and she climbed behind
the wheel, anxious to get back to the Flying B.

But in the evening when she arrived, Jenna entered
the cabin and found J.D. staring into space.

Worried, she asked, "What happened?" He looked
as if someone had just died.

"I know who I am." He turned in her direction, like
a zombie with its heart falling out of its chest. "I remember everything, including the murder of my wife."

Chapter Thirteen

"Your *wife?* Her *murder?*"

J.D. nodded, Jenna's choppy questions echoing in his ears. His memories had come crashing back, shaking him to the core. He'd spent the last few hours holed up in the cabin remembering the most painful things imaginable.

She dropped onto the sofa as if her knees had just buckled.

"Kimie was gunned down at a convenience store," he said, wishing he'd caught Jenna before she'd fallen onto the furniture. She looked as white as death. But it was Kimie who was dead. "There was a robbery in progress when she walked into the store. The gunman panicked and shot her, killing her instantly. Then he turned and fired at the clerk, a young guy who was scared out of his wits and had only worked there for a few weeks." J.D. backed himself against the window, moving away from Jenna instead of toward her, with Kimie's lifeless body floating in his mind. "The clerk survived the injury and served as a witness in court."

"The gunman was apprehended?" Her voice vibrated.

He glanced out the window. The blinds were open, the darkness thick and vast. "He fled the scene, but he didn't get far. He was taken into custody the same night."

"I'm so sorry about your wife." She sounded tearful. "There was a moment, a couple of days ago, that I wondered if you'd been married. But it didn't seem possible. And I never would have thought..."

Was she misty-eyed? He didn't want to look at her to see. "There's nothing you can do. There isn't anything anyone can do."

"I wish there was."

He finally glanced at her. Her eyes *were* damp, and he suspected that she wanted to wrap him in her arms and to try to console him. But he couldn't bring himself to allow it, and she was obviously aware of how unapproachable he was. He stayed plastered against the window.

"When did you lose her?" she asked.

"Two years ago." But it seemed like yesterday, especially with the way his memories had come crashing back.

He glanced at Jenna again. By now she was sitting a little more forward on the sofa, and she looked as discomposed as he felt.

She spoke quietly. "What's your name?"

"Joel. Joel Daniel Newman."

"Do you want me to call you Joel?"

"No. I'm J.D. now. It still works as my initials." He didn't want to be Joel anymore. He'd been that to his wife. "Her full name was Kimie Ann Winters-Newman. We were married for six years. We were happy." His stomach went horribly tight. "I loved her, and she loved me. We were right together. So damned right. The only thing missing in our lives were children. We'd been trying to conceive, but couldn't. Kimie wasn't able to. So we decided to adopt. A whole passel of kids. That was our plan."

Jenna didn't reply, but she was riveted to his every word, gazing at him with her pretty blue eyes.

He went on. "We discovered how difficult it was to adopt an infant and learned how many foster kids were out there, needing homes."

"So the kids who'd been crowding your memories, who'd been left behind, are the ones you were hoping to adopt someday?"

He nodded. "The family that can never be repaired. Kimie and me and our nonexistent children." He paused to temper the quaver in his tone. He couldn't bear to break down in front of Jenna. "We were also looking into foreign adoption. With me being part Cherokee and her being part Japanese, we knew what it would take to raise kids from other cultures. We knew how important it would be to keep them connected to their roots and to teach them about ours." He considered the nickname Jenna had called him. "The sushi cowboy. Kimie would have liked that."

"Is she the tea drinker you were struggling to remember?"

"Yes. She had a cup of herb tea almost every night

before we went to bed. Sometimes I fixed it for her. We had this easy rhythm, knowing each other's habits, catering to them."

She got teary again. "It makes sense now, the reason marriage and babies made you uncomfortable. It wasn't because you couldn't relate to that lifestyle. It's because you mourned it."

He didn't reply, and she went disturbingly quiet, too.

He shattered the silence. "Do you know why your hair fascinated me? Kimie said that some of our kids would be blond. Us with our dark hair, walking around with golden-haired children." Suddenly he wanted to touch Jenna's fair locks, to indulge in each wavy strand. But he stayed where he was. He was confused by his feelings. He shouldn't be thinking about Kimie while he was longing to touch Jenna. It only worsened the pain. "I should have never gotten you involved in my mixed-up life. I should have stayed at the homeless shelter."

"Don't talk like that."

"How else am I supposed to talk?" He could tell that she was confused, too, and that he'd dragged her into something neither of them could handle.

Jenna ached for J.D., but she also hurt for herself. His memories were like a boomerang flying between them.

Back and forth.

What a horrible twist of fate. At one time J.D. had been the ultimate family man, with the qualities from Jenna's list. Only he wasn't emotionally available anymore. His wife was gone, taken from him in a devastating way, and Jenna was sitting on the sidelines, wishing she could heal him, but knowing she couldn't. Telling him that she loved him was futile now.

"Where did you meet Kimie?" she asked, trying to envision him in happier times, trying to help him feel better.

"We went to the same high school. We saw each other around and flirted a little, but we didn't start dating until later."

"How old are you?" There was so much more she wanted to know about him—this man she loved, this man who would never belong to her.

"Thirty-three. I was twenty when Kimie and I first went out, twenty-five when we got married, and thirty-one when she died."

"I'm sorry," she said, not knowing what else to say yet realizing how meaningless those words were to him.

But even so, he moved forward, slowly, and joined her on the sofa. He still seemed dazed and distant, but he was coming out of his shell, at least a little.

"Have you talked to Doc?" she asked.

"Not yet." He exhaled an audible breath. "You're the first person I've told."

She wondered if he would flinch if she touched him. She didn't take the chance. They sat side by side, with no physical contact.

"How did your visit with your dad go?" he asked, as if suddenly becoming aware of where she had been when his memories surfaced.

"It went well. But we don't need to talk about that right now." There was still so much more she didn't know about him. "Why don't you tell me about your parents instead, and your brothers and sisters, if you have any?"

"I don't. But I had a happy childhood."

"Go on," she coaxed.

"My parents ran a horse farm in a small town in the Texas Panhandle, and that's where I grew up. I get my Cherokee blood from my mom. She taught me about our ancestors. She and Dad are good people, kind and loving." He paused. "When they retired, I purchased the farm from them, and they moved to Arizona. I loved that farm. So did Kimie." His voice cracked. "It's where we made our home together. After she died, my parents tried to talk me into going to Arizona and staying at their place, but I couldn't deal with being around anyone, not even them."

"So what did you do?"

"I sold the farm and started drifting. Sometimes I camped out in remote areas, for months at a time, where there wasn't another soul around. And sometimes I stayed at motels, staring at the walls and rarely leaving the room. I drifted all over Texas, going from town to town. Small towns, like the one I'd left behind."

Like Buckshot Hills, she thought. "Do you recall how you were injured?" The injury that had given him amnesia and had brought him to the Flying B. "Was it a carjacking?"

He nodded. "I stopped to help a man and a woman who appeared to be broken down by the side of the road. I was worried about the woman. That someone else might stop and something bad might happen to her. It never occurred to me that they were setting me up for a robbery."

Jenna understood why he'd been so quick to come to the couple's aid. He'd obviously been thinking about Kimie. "Your heart was in the right place."

He didn't comment on his heart. His broken heart, she thought.

He said, "They must have rigged their car so it wouldn't start. I think the woman struck me on the back of the head when I was leaning over the hood. I don't remember the blow itself, but I remember that the man was standing beside me, so he couldn't have been the one who hit me."

"Do you recall waking up?"

He nodded. "But I was too disoriented to think clearly, to contemplate where I was or why my head hurt so damned much."

"How long do you think you were like that before I found you?"

"The robbery took place about three miles from the Flying B Road. But how long I was wandering around is beyond me. They obviously stole my truck. They also got my cell phone, my I.D. and some cash and credit cards from my wallet, but my social-security card is in a safe-deposit box and the bulk of my money is in an investment account. There wasn't any evidence of the account in my belongings, so it's unlikely they know about it. And even if they discovered it existed, they wouldn't have been able to access it without drawing attention to themselves."

"Thank goodness for that. When are you going to call Deputy Tobbs and give him this information and tell him who you are?"

"Tomorrow. I'm too worn out to do it now. I've got too much going on inside me." He scrubbed a hand across his jaw. "How could I have forgotten her, Jenna?"

"Because it was too painful to remember." She stated the obvious, wishing, once again, that she could ease his sorrow, but knowing she couldn't. She'd never felt so helpless or so useless.

"It still seems wrong to have blocked her from my mind. Instead of remembering Kimie, I was falling for you."

Falling…

She'd been falling, too, only with the word *love* attached. J.D. wasn't making that claim. "You didn't do anything wrong. You have a right to keep living."

"I don't want that right. I want to disappear. I want to keep running."

"You can't drift forever."

"Yes, I can. I have enough money in my investment account to keep me going for a long time. And when it runs out, then I'll get ranch jobs, like this one. Temporary work so I don't have to put down roots. I don't ever want to put down roots again. It isn't worth it."

She looked into his eyes, trying to see the man he'd once been. But all she saw was emptiness. Still she said, "Maybe someday you'll feel differently."

He stood up and moved away from the sofa. "I'm going to pay you back for your hospitality, like I wanted to from the beginning."

"You know that doesn't matter to me."

"It matters to me, and now that I know I have money in the bank, I can give you what I owe you."

"If it makes you feel better, go ahead."

"I wonder if I should go to a motel tonight. I have enough cash from my wages for a few nights stay, and I—"

"What? Why?"

"I can't sleep in the same bed with you, Jenna. I wish I could, but after remembering Kimie…"

"Don't leave the ranch. Not this soon. Wait until you talk to Deputy Tobbs and get everything sorted out.

I'll go back to the main house, and you can stay here by yourself."

"Are you sure? I don't want to put you out."

"You aren't putting me out. I wouldn't be staying in the cabin if you weren't here, anyway. Besides, maybe you'll have a comforting dream tonight."

"About Kimie?" His voice jumped. "Do you think that's possible?"

"I don't know. But it's worth a shot."

"Then I'll stay here. Thank you."

Jenna got up, and they gazed awkwardly at each other.

"You've been such a good friend all along," he said. "And you still are."

"I want what's best for you." And sharing his bed wasn't in his best interest, not when he wanted to be alone. "I should pack my things now."

She went into the bedroom, trying to hold herself together, to keep from crying in earnest. Finally she was ready, everything shoved into her suitcases.

He loaded them into her truck. "You look like you're going on a major trip."

But she was only going to another house on the same property. *So close, yet so incredibly far,* she thought. She was going to miss snuggling in J.D.'s arms tonight. She was going to miss him for the rest of her life.

"I'll talk to you tomorrow," he said. "And if you see Doc, will you tell him what's going on and that I'll talk to him tomorrow, too?"

"Of course."

"Night, Jenna."

"Sleep well, J.D."

"I will if I dream. God, I hope I dream."

"I hope so, too." He needed Kimie more than he needed her. Jenna couldn't compete with that. Nor was she going to try.

After hauling her luggage into the house, Jenna confided in Doc and Tammy, who were in the kitchen, where Tammy was baking a boysenberry pie.

Both were genuinely concerned and felt badly that J.D.'s memories had triggered such tragic news. Doc said that he would visit J.D. in the morning, and Tammy gave Jenna a sweet hug.

Later, Jenna talked to Donna. They sat on Jenna's bed in their pajamas, with plates of the leftover pie between them.

"This must be the worst night of your life," Donna said.

"It was a good day until I got home and found out about J.D. I think it's nice that Dad loved Savannah."

"And married Mom on the rebound? What's nice about that?"

"That part upset me, too. But I could tell that Dad had never meant to hurt Mom. And now that I feel about J.D. the way I do, I understand how conflicted Dad was."

"Love isn't an excuse to behave badly."

"No it isn't, but when you're caught up in it, you do things you wouldn't normally do. Who knows? Maybe I'll end up marrying someone on the rebound, too. I mean, honestly, Donna, how am I ever going to love someone the way I love J.D.? It seems impossible to love another man with the same intensity that I feel for him."

"Why do you have to get married at all? What's wrong with staying single?"

Laden with loneliness, Jenna sighed. She'd never told Donna about her list, and now wasn't the time, especially since she couldn't imagine anyone except J.D. fitting the bill. "How am I going to have children if I don't get married?"

"You don't have to be married to have kids. Single women can adopt these days or use a surrogate or go to a sperm bank."

"I know, but I can't picture myself in the role of being a single mom. And none of those methods sounds appealing to me. I want a family the traditional way."

"Then I hope you get what you want someday. I hate seeing you hurt."

"At least I squared things with Dad. He wants you to forgive him, too."

Donna shook her head. "I can't deal with Dad's issues right now."

"He's going to make amends with Uncle William. He's going to call him and apologize."

"Really?" Donna arched a delicate brow. "And whose idea what that? Yours or his?"

"I suggested it, but he agreed fairly easily. We made a pact—I would tell J.D. that I loved him, and he would apologize to William."

"You're not keeping your end of the bargain."

"How can I, knowing what I know about his past?"

"You can't, I guess. But it seems sad for you to keep it a secret. It doesn't seem right for him to stop living, either."

"That's what I told him. Maybe if he has a dream about Kimie, he'll realize that."

"An angel dream?"

"I hadn't thought about it that way. But yes, I suppose so. Kimie would be his angel if she appears to him in a dream."

Donna reached for her hand. "I hope it happens the way you want it to."

The sisterly solace was much needed. Both of them went silent for a while, even after their fingers drifted apart and Jenna managed to stave off her tears, as she'd been doing for most of the night. Donna truly cared, and it truly mattered.

Jenna caught her breath and said, "What I want is for him to love me and want to be with me. Dad said that he couldn't imagine J.D. not being in love with me."

"Dad isn't the authority on love, but I agree, I can't imagine J.D not loving you."

"Thank you. But I actually think Dad is an authority. The way he talked about Savannah. About the way both of them felt about each other."

But it wasn't a comforting thought, considering how their father's life had turned out, and Jenna could only pray that she wasn't destined to follow in his shaky footsteps.

Chapter Fourteen

In the morning, all Jenna could do was think about J.D. and how he was faring. But she wasn't going to go down to the cabin until Doc returned, and Doc was there now.

She looked across the breakfast table at Tammy. Her cousin had fixed the meal—pancakes—and they were waiting together.

Jenna took small bites, trying not to heighten the tightness in her stomach. Earlier she'd questioned Tammy about the preparation of the food. Not because this was the time to continue her cooking lessons, but because she was trying to keep her mind engaged. The batters for pancakes and waffles, she'd learned, were similar but not the same. Traditionally waffle batter was made with egg yolks and the whites were whipped separately and folded in just before cooking. It sounded complicated to her, but at the moment, everything was complicated.

"How are you holding up?" Tammy asked.

"Not well. I—"

The sound of footsteps interrupted their conversation. Doc entered the kitchen, and Jenna nearly knocked over her juice, catching the glass before it fell.

"Did J.D. dream last night?" she blurted, asking him the first thing that popped into her head.

"No, he didn't," Doc replied. "I suggested grief counseling, but he refuses. As you're aware, he was already struggling with this, drifting around aimlessly. But the amnesia has only made things worse."

Jenna understood. Now that J.D. was remembering the details of his wife's death, he was reliving the horror all over again. "I wish he would listen to you and see a grief counselor."

"Maybe you can talk him into it."

"I'll try." She left the table and her pancakes half eaten, but she knew that Tammy didn't mind.

When she arrived at the cabin, J.D. was sitting on one of the mismatched porch chairs, with shadows beneath his eyes. Obviously he'd had a restless night. She'd tossed and turned, too.

"Doc was just here," he said.

"I know. I spoke to him. Why don't you want to get grief counseling?"

"It won't do any good."

"How do you know it won't?"

"Counseling won't bring Kimie back." He frowned into the sun. "Why didn't I dream about her last night? Why didn't she appear to me? I wanted her to, so damned badly."

She wasn't able to answer his questions. "When I told Donna what you were hoping for, she called it an angel dream."

"That's nice. I like that."

"I think so, too." She sat beside him. "And there's still time to dream about her. You can stay at the cabin for as long as you need to."

"What if it doesn't happen?"

"Don't lose hope."

"My hope ended on the day she died. Besides, who am I trying to kid? How is a dream going to help? Even if she came to see me, she would only disappear again."

She didn't know what to say to comfort him. She wasn't able to comfort herself, either.

He left his chair, and the timeworn planks that made up the porch creaked beneath his feet. He stood beside the chipped wood rail, with the Flying B as his backdrop.

Jenna stayed seated and studied him. He was dressed in his original clothes, the jeans and shirt he'd been wearing on the afternoon she'd found him stumbling along the road. His hair was tousled, too, most likely from running his hands through it, also mirroring how he'd looked that day. She'd been attracted to him from the start, but she'd never imagined falling in love with him. Nor could she have predicted what his memories would unveil.

He said, "I called Deputy Tobbs earlier, before Doc came to see me. Now that the police know who I am, they're going to run a search on my stolen credit cards, my cell phone, my vehicle and everything else that might lead them to the carjackers. In the meantime, I need to apply for a temporary license and replacement credit cards. After I get my new ID, I can go to the bank and withdraw the money I owe you. I'm going to get a new cell, too, and buy a used truck."

"Did you contact your bank?"

He nodded. "My investment account is secure, like I assumed it would be."

She couldn't help but ask, "Did you tell Deputy Tobbs about your past? Did you tell him about Kimie?"

"Yes, and he said that he was sorry. That's what people always say."

"Because they are sorry."

"I know. But to me, they've become empty words. I've heard them more times than I could ever count." He changed the subject. "I'm still interested in hearing about your meeting with your dad. Will you tell me about it now?"

"Yes, of course." She relayed the details to him.

"Your Dad and Savannah were in love? None of us saw that coming."

"No, we didn't, and neither did they. Neither of them expected to feel that way about each other." She crossed her arms over her chest, hugging herself in a protective manner. Then she asked, "When did you know that you loved Kimie?"

"I don't recall the exact moment. But it happened easily." He frowned. "Everything came easily to me then. I lived a charmed life. Supportive parents, a thriving horse farm, a great girlfriend that I was looking forward to marrying."

Jenna kept questioning him, her curiosity too intense to ignore. "How did you propose?"

"The usual way, I guess. I bought a ring, took her out

to dinner and popped the question." He smiled a little. "I wasn't nervous because I knew she would say yes."

"Where was the wedding?"

"On the farm." He gazed out at the Flying B. "This would be a nice place for a wedding, too."

Her throat went dry. She could imagine marrying him here. "Donna is working on making it into a wedding location. She's designing a garden with a gazebo for those types of events."

He kept gazing at the ranch. "That sounds pretty."

"It will be."

He turned to look at her. "When I'm gone, I'm going to envision you in the gazebo with your groom by your side, taking the vows you've always wanted to take."

Tears banked her eyes. "And how should I envision you, J.D., drifting from town to town, lonely and filled with despair? You should stay here. You should live on the Flying B and make this your home."

"I can't."

"You could if you wanted to. Hugh would be glad to create a permanent position for you. You're an asset to the ranch."

"It would never work. Besides, it would be weird later when your husband is around."

Her husband? A stranger who no longer mattered? Her resolve snapped. "You're the man I want. *You.* Damn it, I love you, J.D.!" The crimson-hot admission flew out of her mouth so quickly, so violently, it could have been blood.

The image made her think of Kimie, and she flinched from the visual. His wife, dead on the convenience-store floor, soaked in red.

J.D. reacted just as badly. He gripped the railing behind him so tightly he was probably getting splinters from the wood. She waited for him to speak.

When he did, his expression was as taut as his hands. "Don't love me. Please, don't."

"I didn't mean for it to happen."

"Oh, Jenna." He returned to his seat. "You promised you wouldn't get attached." His tone was sad, not accusatory, but that only exaggerated her pain.

"I tried not to."

He leaned forward and put his forehead against hers. Her pulse jumped like a rocket. His skin was incredibly warm, and he was close enough to kiss. She envied Kimie for how desperately he'd loved her. That made Jenna's pain more pronounced, too. Envying a dead woman.

"You and I aren't meant to be," he told her, his breaths whispering across her face.

"I wish we were."

"So do I. But I can't be the man you need."

He pulled back, leaving her bereft. She merely sat there, aware of how broken she must look—glassy-eyed, unblinking.

"I'm sorry," he said, then scoffed at his own words. "Sorry. As if that helps, right?"

"Actually, it does. A little." Unlike him, she longed to be consoled. Regardless, she got to her feet. She couldn't remain on his porch, torturing herself with his presence. "We should probably keep our distance now."

"I'll try to get everything in order as soon as I can. Then I can leave, and you can try to forget that you were ever with me."

She shook her head. "I'll never forget, J.D."

"Nor will I," he replied as she walked away. "Never again."

J.D. followed through. He got his license, his new truck, a cell phone and everything else as quickly as possible. And now, on the day he was leaving, he made a point of saying goodbye to everyone on the ranch. He'd spent the morning with the ranch hands, portions of the afternoon with Doc and Tammy, and now, as dusk neared, he prepared to see Jenna.

He knew she was in the barn, avoiding him and working her tail off. That was mostly what she'd been doing since she'd told him that she loved him.

He never should've started the affair with her. He had no right to mess with her feelings when his had been so damned jumbled. A man with amnesia wasn't what Jenna needed. Of course a man with horrific memories wasn't what she needed, either. He was no good for her, either way.

J.D. entered the barn and headed for the section of the stables that housed the school horses. When he saw her, he released a rough breath. She was cleaning the hooves of one of the new geldings. She looked intent on her task, too intent, too focused. She was well aware that this was the day he was leaving, with no plan to ever come back.

He waited until she finished with the hooves, then he said her name, softer than he should have. "Jenna."

She glanced up, and their gazes met.

"J.D." She spoke his name just as softly.

He moved closer, and she exited the gelding's stall and met him in the breezeway.

"My truck is all packed," he said.

"So this is it?"

"Yes." The end. Their final farewell. "I don't know where I'm going. I'm just going to drive and see where the road takes me."

"It's supposed to rain later. A quick summer storm."

Somehow that seemed fitting. "I can handle the rain."

"Just be careful."

As their conversation faded, he looked around at the barn. They'd never crept out here on a moonlit night to make love. Heaven help him, he still had fantasies of Jenna with hay in her hair. He longed to kiss her good-bye, to feel her lips against his, but he refrained from suggesting it, knowing it would only make his departure more difficult.

Instead he said, "I never did have that dream. But it's probably my own fault for not believing that it would matter, anyway. Or maybe Kimie is just too far away to connect with me." He was beyond trying to figure anything out.

"Did you have any pictures of her in your truck? Did those get stolen, too?"

"I had a photograph in my wallet of the two of us together." So far the police had yet to solve his case, and he doubted that even if his vehicle was recovered, his belongings would still be in it. "But I have more pictures of her. The rest of them are in my safe-deposit box, back in the town where we lived."

She glanced at his hand. "Did you ever wear a wedding ring?"

"I did when she was alive."

"What did you do with it after she died?"

"I buried it with her."

"You buried everything with her—your heart, your soul, your life."

"I know, but I can't cope any other way."

"I think she would want a happier existence for you."

"I spent eleven years with Kimie, five as her boyfriend and six as her husband. Being happy without her isn't in my realm of thinking."

Yet, suddenly, he was worried about missing Jenna as badly as he'd been missing Kimie, and Jenna was still alive, standing right before him and willing to be his partner. But he wouldn't be good for her, he reiterated. She deserved someone new and fresh, not someone damaged from the past.

She said, "You should get going before the rain starts."

Yes, he should. But it wasn't the rain that concerned him. He needed to get away from Jenna before the thought of losing her worsened. He didn't have amnesia anymore, but he was as mixed-up as ever.

"Bye, Jenna."

"Goodbye, J.D. Joel Daniel," she added, using his birth name. "Strange, how I got your initials right."

"You got everything right. It's me that screwed things up."

"That isn't true. I'm the one who fell in love when I wasn't supposed to."

"People can't help falling in love." He took a chance and drew her into his arms, wrapping her in a hug that made him want to stay.

Jenna clutched his shoulders, holding him like a lifeline. Only he wasn't her salvation. Someday, the right man would come along and fill her with joy.

He ended the embrace, and they gazed at each other in a blaze of pain.

He walked away. She didn't follow him, and he didn't glance back to see what she was doing. But he suspected that her eyes were rimmed with tears.

He strode swiftly to his truck, got behind the wheel and steered it in the direction of nowhere, realizing that he was in love with Jenna, too.

Yes, by God, he *loved* her. Still, he didn't turn his vehicle around. He kept going.

Hours later, he drove straight into the rain. He drove and drove, the windshield wipers clapping, washing the water aside, only to have it return again.

As the night got darker and wetter, he squinted at the misty highway. Then, finally, he stopped at an average little motel, ready to rest his weary bones.

And when he crawled into bed, it was with Jenna Byrd on his mind.

Jenna went to bed that night in the dream cabin. She wanted to sleep where J.D. had been sleeping, to inhale his scent on the sheets, to hug a pillow to her body and imagine that he was holding her the way he used to.

As she closed her eyes, she wondered where he was. She missed him beyond reason. But she knew that she would.

She slept fitfully, dozing in and out of repose. But eventually she fell into uninterrupted slumber.

And dreamed.

She saw herself on the Flying B, walking barefoot through the grass, only there were clouds billowing near her feet, hovering just above the ground. She couldn't feel them, but they went on forever, stretching beyond the boundaries of her vision.

She kept walking toward something or someone, uncertain of her final destination.

Then the scene changed, and she was on another ranch. No, not a ranch. A horse-breeding farm. Outdoor pens shimmered with mares and foals, frolicking among the grass-level clouds, which looked more like spun sugar here.

Then she remembered J.D.'s youthful dream and the boy he'd once been, with sugar cubes in his pocket. This was his horse farm, she realized. His old place.

Jenna glanced across the farm and saw a dark-haired woman coming toward her. Kimie. J.D.'s murdered wife. There was no gunshot wound, no blood, nothing to indicate that she was dead, except the sweet heavenly groundcover.

Small and lean with exotic features, Kimie wore a simple ensemble—a denim shirt and blue jeans. Like Jenna, her feet were bare. Only she wasn't alone. She carried a child on her hip. A little girl, no more than two, with wavy blond hair, similar to Jenna's. Clearly, she represented one of the many foster kids Kimie and J.D. had hoped to adopt, and Kimie had chosen her because she was a delicate reminder of why J.D. had become fascinated with Jenna's sunny-colored hair.

Kimie stopped and put the child down, smoothed her pink dress and patted her on the bottom. The toddler smiled and started running toward Jenna, going as fast as her sturdy little legs would go. She tripped and disappeared in the cotton candy clouds. A millisecond later, she popped back up and continued to run.

Instinctively, Jenna got down on her knees and

opened her arms, welcoming the child into her embrace. Scooping her up, she hugged her close.

Kimie didn't come any closer. She watched from afar. Then she lifted her hand in a wave and vanished, an angel returning to her ethereal world and taking the clouds with her.

The little girl said, "Bye-bye," in a tiny voice, making tears come to Jenna's eyes.

The scene changed again, and she and the child were back on the Flying B. Jenna kissed the little girl's cheek, and more children appeared.

Hundreds of them.

They were everywhere, chattering and playing. All ages, all sizes, all nationalities. Every adoptable foster child in Texas was here, she thought, along with potential adoptees from other countries. Kimie had sent them, offering them to Jenna.

But what about J.D.? He was nowhere to be seen.

Still clutching the original girl, Jenna looked for him. The other children helped search, too, running all over the ranch, shouting his name. But no one found him.

Soon Jenna awakened, shrouded in darkness. She reached out to gather the children, but they were gone, even the little one she'd been carrying.

She turned on the light and burst into tears. She wanted to call J.D., but she couldn't. He hadn't given her his number. He was unreachable.

Just like in the dream.

Chapter Fifteen

J.D. woke up with a start. He'd just had the most
vivid dream, only he wasn't in it. But Jenna and Kimie
were, along with scores of kids. They'd been calling
his name at the end of the dream, but he wasn't able to
answer because he wasn't there. He was here, alone in
a pitch-black motel room.

He switched on the lamp and squinted at the invasion
of the light. When he'd hoped for a dream, he'd never
fathomed anything like this—Kimie and Jenna together,
with depictions of the children he and Kimie had lost.

Jenna had looked so natural, holding the toddler in
her arms. And his wife—clever, beautiful Kimie—
making certain that the first child who appeared was
blonde, like Jenna.

It didn't take a psychologist to figure out what it
meant. Kimie was telling J.D. that she approved of

Jenna, as a woman and a future mother, but Kimie wasn't telling J.D. what to do. The choice was his. He could keep drifting or return to Jenna and create a family with her.

Really, it was a no-brainer and something he should have done without Kimie's intervention. But he'd been locked so deeply in his pain, he'd run off, even after he'd acknowledged to himself that he loved Jenna.

He glanced at the clock. It was four in the morning, or nearly four. 3:56 a.m.

He got out of bed. He wanted to call Jenna, but at this ungodly hour? It didn't seem right to rip her from sleep. Still, he wanted to hear her voice, to tell her that he'd made a mistake and that he loved her.

Would she appreciate his dream? Or would she feel slighted that he hadn't come to his senses until after Kimie had appeared?

There was only one way to know. He needed to call her. But he fixed a cup of coffee first, waiting for daylight.

And it was the longest wait of his life. He felt as if he might go mad with it. The numbers on the clock moved so slowly, he considering yelling at them to hurry.

To keep himself occupied, he opened the window and peered outside. The ground was damp with rain, but drops were no longer falling.

The wait continued.

Finally, *finally,* dawn broke through the gray-scattered sky, and he lifted his cell phone from the nightstand and dialed Jenna's cell. It rang and rang, until her voice mail came on. He didn't leave a message; he wanted to talk to her in person.

But he couldn't just sit around until she became available. He was already going stir-crazy. He took a shower and got dressed. Grabbing his bag, he made a beeline for his truck. He was hours away from the Flying B, but by damn, he was going there, as quickly as he could.

Then a terrible thought struck him. What if something deterred him? What if he was in an accident? He knew how quickly the unexpected could happen. Look at Kimie. After a hectic night of birthing foals, she'd dashed down to the corner store to buy a few things. Never in a million years could J.D. have imagined her not coming back.

Or coming back in a box.

His mind drifted to her funeral—the scrolled-wood coffin, the flickering candles, the wreaths of flowers, her family clutching each other and crying. J.D. hadn't cried, not in front of everyone. He'd kept his tears private. But he'd been inconsolable, nonetheless.

There were no guarantees that he was going to live happily-ever-after with Jenna. Something could happen to Jenna as easily as it could happen to him.

The thought of losing her someday nearly sent him into a panic. But he forced himself to breathe. He was sitting in the parking lot, obsessing about the darkness associated with death, even after he'd seen an angelic version of Kimie in a dream.

Doc had been right. J.D. needed grief counseling.

And he needed to leave Jenna a message, too, to tell her that he loved her, just in case he never made it back to the ranch. He dialed the number again, preparing for her voice mail. But Jenna answered.

"Hello?" she said in the customary way, and her voice was the most beautiful sound he'd ever heard.

"It's me," he replied. "J.D."

"Oh, my God." She gasped. "I'm so glad it's you. I slept in the dream cabin last night, and I had a dream where I was searching for you. Kimie was there in the beginning, and she…"

Jenna went on to describe the dream J.D. had experienced. Every detail was exact. Wonderfully astounded, he listened while she relayed every moment.

Afterward, he said, "Me, too."

"You, too, what?"

"I had the same dream."

The shock in her voice was evident. "You did?"

"Identical. I woke up with you and the kids calling my name." He told her his interpretation of it. Then he said, "I love you, Jenna, and I shouldn't have walked away. I knew that I loved you when I left. But I was scared. I'm still scared."

"Of what?"

"Losing each other."

"We aren't going to lose each other, J.D. We belong together."

"I belonged with Kimie, too, and look what happened to her." He paused to quell his shiver. "I'm going to get the grief counseling Doc recommended. I know I need it."

"Maybe that's the most important message Kimie was trying to convey."

That until he found himself, no one could find him, either? "I'm going to learn to tackle my fears, and I want to be with you while I'm working on it. I want to be with you for as long as God allows."

"Then come to me. Come home now."

"I will. I am." He started his engine, destined for the Flying B.

Jenna waited for J.D. at the dream cabin. In fact, she sat on the porch, wanting to see his truck as it rolled up.

Hours later, he was there, climbing out of his vehicle and coming toward her. She held out her arms, and he enfolded her in his. They held each other so tightly, air whooshed from her lungs, but she didn't care. All that mattered was that they were together.

He kissed her, and she melted from the feeling. It was the most powerful kiss they'd exchanged, the connection warm and soulful. When it ended, they caressed each other's faces, fingers gliding over familiar features.

"Will you marry me?" he asked. "Not right away. After I get the counseling I need."

Her heart soared. "You know I will."

He flashed his crooked grin. "And adopt hundreds of children with me?"

She laughed. She knew he was referring to the kids in the dream. "I don't think Kimie meant for us to take all of them. But we'll adopt as many as we can."

He lowered a hand to her stomach. "I'm going to plant some babes in your womb, too." He grinned again. "You're going to be one busy little mama."

"And you'll be a busy papa."

"Maybe we really will end up with hundreds of them."

"Goodness, can you imagine?"

"Not really, no." But he was still grinning. "We can

use my money to build a house. A big, kid-friendly house."

"On the Flying B," she added. "There's plenty of room for us to put down roots here."

"We should have the ceremony on the ranch, too. In the garden and gazebo Donna is designing. Ours will be the first Flying B wedding."

"Unless Doc and Tammy beat us to it."

He shrugged. "It's okay if they do. They already have a jump start on the engagement. But it's going to be fun to plan our wedding. 'Let's Make Love' is going to be our song."

"It already is." It was from the moment they'd danced to it at Lucy's. "I'll wear a long silky dress and those old-fashioned western boots. The kind that lace up the front."

"That works for me. I can already see you in my mind. The elegant country bride."

She thought about his other wife. The lovely young woman in the dream. The lady who'd blessed them with the gift of hope. "What did Kimie wear when you married her?"

"Her dress had a Japanese flair. Her mother made it for her. My mom got involved, too, and beaded a Native design on my jacket. I can show you the pictures from our wedding album when I go to my safe-deposit box and bring everything here."

"I'd love to see them." She was thrilled that he was able to talk about Kimie in a positive way. It was a good start and was only going to get better. "Do you think your parents are going to like me?"

"Are you kidding? They're going to adore you, and they're going to be grateful that I'm not drifting all over

Texas any more. I know they've been praying for me to make a new life."

"And now you are."

"Because of you." He looped her into his arms again. "I'm going to make sure that our bed is filled with rose petals on our wedding night. I want to make that fantasy happen for you."

"You still owe me a naughty night in the barn, too."

"I know. I thought about that when I left the ranch. How we hadn't done it. How I'd been missing out on seeing you with hay in your hair." He nuzzled her cheek. "We could do it tonight."

Sweet chills shimmied up and down her spine. She couldn't imagine a more romantic homecoming. She wanted to do luscious things with J.D.

Tonight, and every night thereafter.

They slipped into an empty stall at midnight, and J.D. spread a blanket on the ground. He'd brought a battery-operated lantern, too. He kept it on low, so it shone gently.

Jenna stood quietly, watching him with a loving expression, her hair tumbling over her shoulders and her dress flowing around booted ankles. She'd deliberately worn something that would be easy to remove, and he knew that she was naked underneath.

This was their moment. Their fantasy.

He extended his hand, and she came forward, joining him on the blanket. They kissed soft and slow, immersed in a bond only lovers could share.

He lifted her dress above her head. She'd become everything to him, everything good and pure. His future wife. The mother of his future children. The woman who loved him enough to help him heal.

J.D. didn't get undressed all the way. He merely opened his shirt and undid his pants.

"That's cheating," she said.

"Not if someone happens by. I can right myself real quick."

She lay there, all sweet and seductive, bare, except for her boots. Looking up at him, she asked, "What about me?"

"You, I'll wrap in the blanket."

"And ruin my good-girl reputation? That's not fair." But she was smiling as she said it.

"Your reputation won't be ruined." He smiled, too. "I'm going to marry you, remember? Right here on the ranch." He realized that he'd omitted a significant part of the wedding plans. "Do you want to shop for a ring tomorrow?" He held her hand up to the light. "A diamond we can pick out together."

"Of course I want to shop with you."

"We'll go bright and early. I want you to have a ring as soon as possible." To reflect their commitment and symbolize their unity. "God gave me a second chance to be with someone I love."

"And He gave me the man from my list." She pressed her lips to his ear. "I can't show it to you, not at the moment. But I can tell you what's on it."

Talk about sexy, whispering to him about her infamous list. "Yes, ma'am, you can. But I'm already familiar with some of it." Things she'd mentioned over the course of their affair. He recited what he knew. "You want an honest, marriage-minded, family oriented man who shares your love of horses and embraces the Flying B as his home."

"So far so good." She tugged him closer. "Chivalry is high on my priorities. Kindness, too. He must be giving and caring."

"That's understandable. Is there more?"

"Strong work ethic. Integrity. I also appreciate a man who has a sense of humor."

"Do you?" He circled her nipples, coaxing them into pearly pink nubs. "Because I seem to recall my sense of humor grating on you."

She made a breathy sound. "Yours is exceptionally wicked. It took some getting used to."

"Glad we cleared that up." He caressed her curves, up, down and all around. "What else?"

She leaned into him. "His physical attributes—tall, dark and handsome."

"That's a cliché."

"Not to me. I'm partial to dark hair and dark eyes."

He slipped his fingers between her legs and elicited a moan. "Anything else?"

"A man who knows how to make me…"

"Make you what?"

"Orgasm."

"You're a bad girl for including that." He sent her a dastardly smile. He'd always wondered if she'd put her sexual preferences on it. He'd even teased her in that regard, just as he couldn't help teasing her now, rubbing her most sensitive spot. "A very bad girl."

She arched under his ministrations. "If I'm going to spend the rest of my life with someone, he needs to know what's what."

He heightened the foreplay. "Like this?"

"Yes, just like that."

He continued to pleasure her, with his hands, his mouth. In response, she tunneled her fingers through his hair and lifted her hips, rife with sensual energy.

When he gave her the Big O, she muffled her excitement, biting down on her bottom lip to keep from crying out.

J.D. couldn't be more aroused. He snagged the condom from his pocket, shoved his jeans down, sheathed himself and entered her, full and deep. He made damned sure that they rolled off the blanket, too, and she got bits of hay in her hair.

They made love in a fever, each touch wild and thrilling. Heat pounded in his loins. Need shivered through his veins. She kissed him so hard, he dragged her on to his lap, encouraging her to ride him to completion.

Afterward, they collapsed in a heap of tangled limbs. Once they were able to move, she put her dress back on, and he fastened his clothes.

Quietly, they returned to the dream cabin. Not to dream, but to sleep. The new couple. In each other's arms.

Where they belonged.

A week later, Jenna, Tammy and Donna went into town, where they met with Roland Walker for an update. He told him exactly what he'd been doing to search Savannah, and even though he still didn't have any news of her, he was convinced that he would locate her. Roland was a confident man.

He was also a tad gruff, but Jenna liked him. She understood why Tex had hired him at one time, too. The P.I. was a good old boy, much like Tex had been.

Jenna considered Tex and his sons. By now, Dad had apologized to Uncle William, and they were working on making amends. They'd even planned a fishing trip.

She glanced over at Tammy. Her cousin was glad, of course, that their dads were trying to be brothers. Jenna was, too. But Donna hadn't said much about it.

After their meeting with Roland, they stopped by the local ice-cream parlor, shared a cafe table and ate dessert. Tammy got two scoops of vanilla, smothered in fruit toppings and colorful sprinkles, Jenna went for a banana split and Donna got frozen yogurt.

Donna, always the odd girl out.

Jenna and Tammy were both engaged and living at the Flying B, the future B and B, with their men. But Donna was busting her butt to get the heck out of Texas and return to New York, where she would continue to work day and night, trying to resume her city-girl career.

It made Jenna feel guilty for being so happy, so settled. The marquee-cut diamond on her finger was dazzling, and she was elated to have it. Tammy had a gorgeous engagement ring, too.

Again, Donna with nothing.

"I have something I want to show you," Jenna said to her sister. She reached into her purse and handed over her list.

Donna began reading. "What in the world is this?"

Jenna explained when she'd first written it, how she'd revised it to include the Flying B, how important it was to her, how J.D had called it her magic and finally, how J.D. turned out to have every single quality she'd imagined in a man.

"That's wonderful," her sister said, "but I don't see how this has anything to do with me."

"I wanted you to see it because I wanted you to be part of it somehow. But I was also hoping that it would inspire you. Not to find a husband, necessarily, but to find whatever it is you need to be joyful."

"Really? Oh." Donna hugged the list close to her heart. "No one has ever said anything like that to me before."

"I should have said it a long time ago. You're my sister, and I love you."

Was Donna holding back tears? She blinked her glamorous lashes, a bit too rapidly. "I love you, too."

Tammy smiled around her next bite. Then she said, "Can I get in on some of that love?"

Jenna grinned and leaned toward her cousin. "Of course you can. Tex knew exactly what he was doing when he brought us together. We're the best trio ever."

"We absolutely are." Tammy ate more ice cream to celebrate.

Jenna glanced at Donna. "You know, sis. It's okay if you secretly want a husband."

Donna shook her head. She laughed a little laugh. "Seriously, Jenna. Where do you come up with this stuff?"

"Most women want to get married someday."

"I'm not most women."

That was true, but still…

"Well, whatever it is you want, I hope you attain it."

"Thank you. That means a lot to me. But all I want is to get my career back on track."

Following Tammy's lead, Jenna attacked the ice cream in her dish. Then she said to Donna, "Since J.D.

and I aren't staying at the dream cabin anymore, you
can sleep there now if you want."

"Whatever for?"

"To have a life-altering dream."

"I think I'll let nature take its course." Donna returned the list. "Why did you move out of the cabin?"

"It doesn't make sense for us to horde it." They were
living in the main house while he was working on the
plans for their custom home. In fact, he was going to
hire Aidan and Nathan to build it. "We have everything we need."

"I'm happy for you," Donna told her. She turned to
Tammy. "And you, too."

Jenna tucked the paper back into her purse. Donna
might not want a husband, but that was what Jenna
wanted for her.

Eventually.

For now, a hot fling with a sinful playboy would do.
She smiled to herself. Maybe after Caleb returned from
his leave of absence, he would take Donna for a sexy
spin. Then later, she could marry the right man, a polished New Yorker or whatever.

"We better get back to the ranch soon," Donna said.
"I've got a slew of work to do."

Yep, Jenna thought, *if anyone needed a little fun, it
was my sister.*

A short while later Donna got her wish and they were
back at the ranch, each going her own way.

Jenna met up with J.D., where he'd just turned some
horses out into the arena, and he rewarded her with a
tender kiss. Although he was making great strides on
his own, he was scheduled to begin his grief counseling

soon. Determined, Jenna thought, to keep his fears at bay and live life to the fullest. She couldn't be prouder.

Luckily, the robbery was behind him, too. The police had arrested the offenders, discovering that they were part of a carjacking ring that had been committing similar crimes all over the country. J.D. had already pressed charges, and Jenna was glad it was over.

In the quiet, they both turned toward the arena and watched the equine activity.

Then J.D. said, "How would you feel if I went back to breeding horses? Not a full-time operation, but just enough to bring some of my expertise to the Flying B. After the B and B is underway and after our house is built."

"I think that's a great idea." She remembered the precious foals she'd seen in the dream at his previous farm. "Mares and their babies."

"To go with Mama Jenna and our babies." He reached out and cradled her in his arms.

She put her head against his shoulder, and they stood in the sun, a wondrous future unfolding before them.

* * * * *

*Look for the final book in the
Byrds of a Feather miniseries
MADE IN TEXAS!
By Crystal Green
Coming in May 2013*

REQUEST YOUR FREE BOOKS!

2 FREE NOVELS PLUS 2 FREE GIFTS!

HARLEQUIN®

SPECIAL EDITION

Life, Love & Family

YES! Please send me 2 FREE Harlequin® Special Edition novels and my 2 FREE gifts (gifts are worth about $10). After receiving them, if I don't wish to receive any more books, I can return the shipping statement marked "cancel." If I don't cancel, I will receive 6 brand-new novels every month and be billed just $4.49 per book in the U.S. or $5.24 per book in Canada. That's a savings of at least 14% off the cover price! It's quite a bargain! Shipping and handling is just 50¢ per book in the U.S. and 75¢ per book in Canada.* I understand that accepting the 2 free books and gifts places me under no obligation to buy anything. I can always return a shipment and cancel at any time. Even if I never buy another book, the two free books and gifts are mine to keep forever.

235/335 HDN FVTV

Name	(PLEASE PRINT)	
Address		Apt. #
City	State/Prov.	Zip/Postal Code

Signature (if under 18, a parent or guardian must sign)

Mail to the Harlequin® Reader Service:
IN U.S.A.: P.O. Box 1867, Buffalo, NY 14240-1867
IN CANADA: P.O. Box 609, Fort Erie, Ontario L2A 5X3

Want to try two free books from another line?
Call 1-800-873-8635 or visit www.ReaderService.com.

* Terms and prices subject to change without notice. Prices do not include applicable taxes. Sales tax applicable in N.Y. Canadian residents will be charged applicable taxes. Offer not valid in Quebec. This offer is limited to one order per household. Not valid for current subscribers to Harlequin Special Edition books. All orders subject to credit approval. Credit or debit balances in a customer's account(s) may be offset by any other outstanding balance owed by or to the customer. Please allow 4 to 6 weeks for delivery. Offer available while quantities last.

Your Privacy—The Harlequin® Reader Service is committed to protecting your privacy. Our Privacy Policy is available online at www.ReaderService.com or upon request from the Harlequin Reader Service.

We make a portion of our mailing list available to reputable third parties that offer products we believe may interest you. If you prefer that we not exchange your name with third parties, or if you wish to clarify or modify your communication preferences, please visit us at www.ReaderService.com/consumerchoice or write to us at Harlequin Reader Service Preference Service, P.O. Box 9062, Buffalo, NY 14269. Include your complete name and address.

HSE13

***

Murphy, please don't get into more trouble.

Whatever had made her think she could be a better parent to Murphy than his other options? He needed a man around, not just a woman he could barely tolerate.

He needed his father.

And now all they had was each other.

Isabella Lockhart couldn't bear to think about it.

"It was an accident!" Murphy yelled. "Dude! That's my bat. You can't just take my bat!"

"I just did, *dude*," the man returned flatly. He closed his hand over Murphy's thin shoulder and forcibly moved him away from Isabella.

Isabella rounded on the man, gaping at him. He was wearing a faded brown ball cap and aviator sunglasses that hid his eyes. "Take your hand off him! Who do you think you are?"

"The man your boy decided to aim at with his blasted baseball." His jaw was sharp and shadowed by brown stubble and his lips were thinned.

"I did not!" Murphy screamed right into Isabella's ear.

She winced, then pointed. "Go sit down."

She drew in a calming breath and turned her head into the breeze that she'd begun to suspect never died here in Weaver, Wyoming, before facing the man again. "I'm Isabella Lockhart," she began.

"I know who you are."

She'd been in Weaver only a few weeks, but it really was a small town if people she'd never met already knew who she was.

"I'm sure we can resolve whatever's happened here, Mr. uh—?"

"Erik Clay."

Focusing on the woman in front of him was a lot safer than focusing on the skinny black-haired hellion sprawled on Ruby's bench.

She tucked her white-blond hair behind her ear with a visibly shaking hand. Bleached blond, he figured, considering the eyes that she turned toward the back of his truck were such a dark brown they were nearly black.

Even angry as he was, he wasn't blind to the whole effect. Weaver's newcomer was a serious looker.

**

Don't miss A WEAVER VOW
by USA TODAY *bestselling author Allison Leigh.*

Available in May 2013 from
Harlequin® Special Edition® wherever books are sold.

HSEEXP0413

HARLEQUIN®

SPECIAL EDITION

Life, Love and Family

EXPECTING FORTUNE'S HEIR
by Cindy Kirk

Shane Fortune is accustomed to women using his
family for money, so when the cute and spunky
Lia Serrano tells him that she is pregnant with his
baby after a one-night stand, he is seriously skeptical.
But after spending more time together, he can't help
but hope the baby is truly his....

Look for the next book in
The Fortunes of Texas:
Southern Invasion

Available in May from Harlequin Special Edition,
wherever books are sold.

MADE IN TEXAS!
by Crystal Green

After inheriting a share of property, independent woman Donna Byrd came to Texas to build a B and B. She'd help market the inn then head right back to her city life…at least, that was the plan until she met cowboy Caleb Granger!

Look for the next story in the *Byrds of a Feather* miniseries next month.

Available in May 2013 from Harlequin Special Edition, wherever books are sold.

It all starts
with a kiss

Check out the brand-new series

HARLEQUIN® KISS™

Fun, flirty and sensual romances.
ON SALE JANUARY 22!

Visit www.tryHarlequinKISS.com
and fall in love with
Harlequin® KISS™ today!